Hide and Seek

Ariana Jones
Book 7

Stacy Claflin

HIDE AND SEEK
ARIANA JONES #7
by Stacy Claflin
http://www.stacyclaflin.com

Copyright ©2025 Stacy Claflin. All rights reserved.
©Cover Design: Didi Wahyudi
Edited by Staci Troilo

This is a work of fiction. Any resemblance to actual persons living or dead, businesses, events, or locales is purely coincidental or used fictitiously. The author has taken great liberties with locales including the creation of fictional towns.

Reproduction in whole or part of this publication without express written consent is strictly prohibited. Do not upload or distribute ebook version anywhere.

Receive free books from the author sign up here: https://stacyclaflin.com/newsletter/

Contents

Chapter 1	1
Chapter 2	5
Chapter 3	10
Chapter 4	14
Chapter 5	18
Chapter 6	23
Chapter 7	28
Chapter 8	33
Chapter 9	37
Chapter 10	42
Chapter 11	47
Chapter 12	51
Chapter 13	55
Chapter 14	59
Chapter 15	64
Chapter 16	68
Chapter 17	73
Chapter 18	77
Chapter 19	83
Chapter 20	87
Chapter 21	92
Chapter 22	98
Chapter 23	102
Chapter 24	106
Chapter 25	110
Chapter 26	114
Chapter 27	119
Chapter 28	123
Chapter 29	127
Chapter 30	132
Chapter 31	136

Chapter 32	141
Chapter 33	145
Chapter 34	148
Chapter 35	153
Chapter 36	157
Chapter 37	161
Chapter 38	165
Chapter 39	169
Chapter 40	173
Chapter 41	180
Chapter 42	186
Chapter 43	190
Books by Stacy Claflin	195
About Stacy Claflin	201
Find Me	203

Chapter One

Snow feathered across the windshield, and Ariana sat up straight, suddenly wide awake after nearly drifting to sleep. "Do you see the snow?"

Damon, who was driving, laughed. "I'd have to be blind to miss it."

Her heart raced. "But the app didn't say anything about snow."

"We're crossing the mountains." He squeezed her knee. "I'd be surprised if there *wasn't* snow."

She looked out the windows. Nothing seemed to be sticking.

"You know what I mean. There was only supposed to be snow on the mountains. The Department of Transportation makes sure those roads are passable. This area is so rural, they might not have a snow plow."

"I'm sure they do. It'll be fine. Why don't you get some sleep? It'll be a while before we get to the restaurant for dinner."

Ari studied the floating snowflakes. "I'm not sure I'll be able to get any rest now."

They had hours of driving ahead of them. While usually she didn't mind the distance, the snow changed everything. Especially with her carrying precious cargo. The whole world seemed so much more dangerous now. That was why they were planning a weekend alone before the chaos of Christmas with family, before morning sickness hit, and before fatigue stole her from their plans for a while. It would be one last hurrah before everything changed for the better.

"Would it help if I went over the packing list again? We have brand new brakes, all-weather tires, and chains in the back. Not to mention enough snacks to feed an army."

"Still, we should've flown. I don't know why I thought driving was a good idea."

"Because we done this before and it was fine?"

She sighed.

"We could always turn around and book a flight," he said with just enough playfulness to brush aside the undercurrent of worry she felt. "Or teleport. Magic portal."

She laughed weakly. "Anything would be better than an hours' long drive over mountains in December."

Damon gave her a knowing look. "You're the one who insisted on the scenic route."

"That was before the clouds turned into a death omen."

"It's flurries, and barely that." He squinted at the sky, pretending fear even though his voice stayed warm. "Look at that. It's horror-movie snow, Ari."

But as he said it, the flakes thickened, no longer drifting—they dove, sharp and fast, the first signs of a storm she hadn't seen in the forecast. His smile faltered for a moment. "Hey, we're okay. I've driven through worse."

His grip on the wheel tightened, and she could practically

feel the thoughts circling behind his eyes. Or maybe she was reading her own nerves into his determined gaze.

She exhaled, tension draining. When he looked at her again, his worry had retreated, replaced by that crooked grin she'd fallen for so long ago.

"Besides," he said, "you're stuck with me all weekend. Storm or no storm. You have no escape."

She rested a hand on her lower stomach, smiling. "Trust me. I wouldn't want one."

His eyes softened in the way that made her heart ache with love and fear twined together. "Are you feeling okay?"

"So far, yes. Ask me again tomorrow morning. I might be cursing the word 'breakfast.' It's only a matter of time before morning sickness hits. I'm surprised it hasn't yet. Rita's hit much earlier than this."

"I'll bring you ginger tea in bed," he promised. "And saltines and anything else you need."

"And you'll pretend not to freak out every time I sneeze." She raised an eyebrow playfully.

"Hey, I only freaked out that one time. I'm never going to hear the end of it, am I?"

"Damon, you thought sneezing was a miscarriage symptom."

"It sounded violent," he quipped.

She chuckled, then fell silent as a harsh gust of wind shoved against the car, just enough to make her brace a hand on the dashboard.

The snow was now falling faster and thicker. Sheets of white engulfed the road, the trees, everything. The world beyond the headlights blurred into a shifting wall of gray.

Damon tapped the steering wheel. "Okay, that escalated quickly."

Ariana's pulse ticked faster. "Do we need to stop?"

"There's nowhere to pull over yet, but I will as soon as I can if this doesn't let up. Promise."

"Okay." She trusted him more than anyone. Still, unease crept through her chest. The storm didn't feel normal. It felt too sudden, like something was closing in.

Damon leaned forward, jaw tight, scanning for any sign of the shoulder. Snow hammered the windshield, thick as handfuls of feathers. "Can you check the GPS? Make sure we're still on the main road?"

His voice was level, but tension threaded through it now.

She reached for her phone, her fingers trembling before she even registered the fear. The screen flickered. Lost signal. Because of course it was.

"No signal."

He cursed under his breath.

Outside, the wind howled, low and mournful—like a warning.

Damon gave her a reassuring smile. "We'll be fine."

But something in her gut whispered that this storm wasn't the only thing coming for them.

Chapter Two

The detour sign appeared out of nowhere. A reflective orange diamond half-covered by tree branches, tilting at an awkward angle as if another storm had shoved it there.

Damon slowed, squinting through the whiteout. "Bridge closed and washout risk. Perfect."

Ariana followed his gaze. The main highway curved ahead into darkness, but the detour arrow pointed sharply right, toward a narrow side road she hadn't noticed on the GPS's map.

"There's no alternate route," she said, refreshing the screen even though she already knew. "Everything's still out."

"It has to link back up. We'll go slow." Damon hesitated only a breath before turning onto the smaller road.

But slow didn't help when the storm quickly covered everything. The trees pressed close on either side—tall, dark silhouettes blurred by wind and snowfall. The road beneath them felt less like asphalt and more like packed powder. Ariana braced a hand on the dash, her pulse picking up with every slide of the tires. "Damon..."

"I know. I'll stop if necessary."

A faint red glow appeared through the storm ahead. Brake lights. Damon eased up beside the vehicle, a compact sedan sitting diagonally across the road, hazard lights blinking weakly through the swirling white.

A young woman stood beside it, bundled in a thin coat far too light for mountain storms. Her dark, tangled hair stuck to her cheeks as she waved frantically at them.

Damon rolled down the window only an inch. "Are you hurt?"

"No," she gasped. "I tried to drive through the drift and now my car's stuck. And the road ahead..." She pointed shakily into the storm. "There's a gap. A whole section's missing."

Ariana's breath caught. "*Missing?*"

"It looks like a bridge collapsed. Or washed out. I don't know. I barely stopped in time!"

Damon shot Ariana a grim, resolved look before putting their SUV in park. "Ari, stay here. I'll take a quick look."

She grabbed his sleeve. "Damon—"

"I'll be careful." His voice was steady, but she heard what simmered beneath it. Fear of the unknown and of losing control, but he still stepped out into the storm.

Ariana watched him through the windshield, her fingers curling tight around her seatbelt. He and the woman, who couldn't have been more than twenty-one, moved to where the road should have continued, their silhouettes barely visible through the snow even with their headlights shining.

Moments later Damon returned, face pale, snow coating his hair and jacket. He shook the ice from his collar before climbing back in.

"She's right," he said quietly. "It's gone. I don't know if it was the storm or something else, but we're not getting across."

"Can we backtrack to the highway?"

"She says it's already blocked. A couple cars slid into each other across the turn. That's how she ended up this way" He exhaled hard. "We're boxed in."

The young woman approached the window again, hugging herself against the cold. Damon lowered it a crack.

"There were other cars behind me," she said. "Two of them pulled over when they saw the drift. We tried calling for help, but nobody has service. There's no way to reach anyone." She pointed behind her, beyond the curve of the narrow road. "But there's a building with a few lights on. Looks like maybe a hospital?"

Ariana straightened, peering through the snow. And there it was—a faint glow, ghostly and pale, barely rising through the storm. "A hospital? Out here?"

"I think so," the young woman said. "It's the only shelter I can see."

Damon and Ariana exchanged a glance. What other choice did they have?

"Tell the other drivers to follow us," Damon said. "We'll head for the hospital together. There's safety in numbers."

Ariana hoped he was right. They'd been through enough to know people weren't always trustworthy. But if they were all travelers stuck, chances were they all just wanted to get to their destinations and nothing more.

The young woman frowned. "I'm going to need a ride. Do you have room? My name's Lana, by the way."

"Nice to meet you, Lana," Damon said. "I'm Damon and this is my wife, Ariana. I wish we could give you a ride, but we're completely packed. I can help you take your belongings to one of the other cars, if they have room."

She didn't look sure, but agreed.

He gave Ari a quick kiss before hefting a couple bags from Lana's car and disappearing into the night.

As they disappeared into the storm, unease prickled across Ariana's arms despite the car's warmth. She should've gone with them. She'd give it ten minutes before going after them.

He returned in nine and a half. The others must not have been far from the stranded car.

Damon quickly closed the door behind him and rested a hand on hers. "You okay?"

"Yeah, just..." She swallowed. "A hospital at night in a storm. It feels like the beginning of one of our podcast episodes."

"That's comforting." Damon started the car moving again. "Worst case, we wait out the storm in a lobby with bad coffee."

But Ariana couldn't shake the sensation threading through her chest. Recognition.

Something about that hospital—its isolation, its dim lights cutting through the blizzard—and the timing felt wrong. Abandoned and alive at the same time.

Behind them, a pair of headlights emerged. Then another. A small caravan of stranded travelers forming in the storm.

"Whatever this place is," Damon said quietly, as the looming building took up more of the horizon, "it's all we've got."

Ariana kept her eyes on the wavering lights ahead, her breath fogging the glass.

She doubted any of them realized what they were driving toward.

Hopefully her mind was on overdrive. She and Damon *did* do work with the most horrific scenarios, so it wasn't hard to jump to the worst conclusions—especially after everything they'd lived through.

Hide and Seek

Maybe this would just be a few ragtag strangers spending the night in a hospital before the storm broke.

Chapter Three

The hospital emerged from the storm in pieces, from the faint glow of floodlights, then the tall rectangular outline of the building, and finally the nearly empty parking lot stretching out like a frozen plain. The wind had carved drifts across the asphalt, covering lines, curbs, everything.

Much more of this, and everything would be covered soon.

Damon eased their SUV into the lot, tires crunching through untouched snow. The lights along the exterior flickered weakly, as if the whole place ran on a generator held together with duct tape and despair.

Ariana leaned forward, squinting. "It doesn't look... open."

"Or maintained."

The others followed slowly behind them. Two vehicles, huddled together like lost animals seeking warmth. Headlights cut through the storm in shaky beams before winking out as the engines turned off.

Ariana's gaze snagged on a shape near the far edge of the lot—a small sedan hidden by fresh snow. Only part of the driver's side door was visible, the rest buried. A long-abandoned car? Hard to tell.

Damon noticed her staring. "Probably abandoned, like the rest of this place."

"Or it could've been left here recently. What if someone is in there waiting for us?"

"For *us*?"

She shrugged, though the distinction mattered. Either way, someone had left the car there.

Lana, the young woman from the stranded sedan trudged toward them, hugging herself against the wind. She wasn't alone now—behind her came a man in his fifties with a bulky jacket and a knit cap pulled low, followed by a couple and their teen daughter. The teen didn't bother shielding herself from the storm. Instead, she glared at the building as if it had personally offended her.

Everyone clustered near the SUV as soon as Damon opened the door.

The older man spoke first, raising his voice over a blast of wind. "Road's a mess behind us. Drift's already blocking my tires. We're not getting out tonight."

His voice was friendly enough, but something about the slow, calculating way he appraised the hospital made Ariana tuck her chin deeper into her scarf.

"What's your name?" Damon asked.

"Reed," the man said. "I'm a truck driver by trade. Long haul. On vacation now. Was trying to beat the storm to get home, but..." He gestured at the whiteout with a helpless shrug.

Ariana forced a polite smile. "I'm Ariana. This is my husband, Damon."

"Nice to meet you both." Reed's gaze lingered on the hospital again, thoughtful. "Strange place to leave empty. Looks newer than I'd have expected."

"Does it?" Damon asked.

Reed shrugged. "Just an observation."

Ari glanced over at the building. "How are we going to get inside?

Lana stepped closer, shivering visibly. "I'll go look."

She ran off before anyone could respond.

"Better not let her be alone." Reed hurried after her.

Damon nudged Ariana. "I'm not sure I trust him. Mind if I go with them to make sure she's okay?"

"Go." She shivered, and he followed them.

The couple approached next. The father, broad-shouldered and red-cheeked, offered a quick nod. "Eric. This is my wife Wendy, and our daughter Kaylee."

Kaylee didn't bother acknowledging anyone. She kept staring at the building, jaw set, earbuds visible even through her thick, dark hair.

Lana arrived back first. "I checked the front doors—they're unlocked. At least, one of them is."

Ariana's stomach tightened. "Unlocked?"

"Yeah. It was cracked open a bit." Lana pulled her hood tighter. "Didn't hear anyone inside, though."

Reed and Damon returned. Damon glanced around the deserted lot, his breath fogging in the cold. "It's not safe staying out here. We need to get into the shelter."

"Storm's getting worse," Wendy said, her voice sharp with worry. "We need shelter now."

Another gust slammed into them, making Ariana stagger.

Damon caught her by the arm, steadying her. "You okay?"

"Yes," she said quickly, though her pulse hammered. The cold cut through her coat, biting at her skin. "We should go in."

Everyone seemed to silently agree. Strength in numbers. Safety in walls, even strange ones.

Reed turned toward the looming entrance. "Let's get inside before the storm buries us."

Everyone grabbed at least one bag before trudging together through knee-deep snow toward the front doors. On the way, Ariana cast one last look at the abandoned car half-covered at the edge of the lot.

For one terrible second, a shape appeared inside the iced-over windshield. A shadow slumped in the driver's seat.

She blinked hard.

Gone. Imagined. Or hidden by snow.

Damon touched her back gently. "Ari?"

"I'm fine. Let's go."

But as they went inside one by one, Ariana felt the unmistakable prickle of warning along her spine.

Whatever drove them inside this hospital, it wasn't just the storm. Deep in that old, scarred place inside her, she had a nagging feeling...

Once they crossed the threshold, getting out again wouldn't be quite so simple.

Chapter Four

A stale, cold draft rolled out, carrying the faintest hint of bleach and something metallic underneath. Not blood. Not necessarily.

Damon stepped in first, shoulders tense. Head on a swivel, he scanned every corner, every exit, every shadow. She followed closely, Lana behind her, Reed and the family trailing last. Snow clung to everyone's clothing in melting patches.

The hospital lobby stretched wide, illuminated only by a scattered patchwork of lights. Some flickered overhead, while others glowed steady but weak, humming with generator fatigue. Half the space was cast in darkness. The reception desk loomed to the right, a purse sitting next to the computer monitor. Abandoned. It didn't have any dust, which meant it was left there recently.

Reed picked up a phone and listened. "It's dead. Not that I'm surprised."

Ariana's pulse gave a quick, sharp kick. "Someone left in a hurry."

Damon nodded. "Or they're still here."

Wendy pulled her teen daughter closer. "Let's not jump to conclusions."

Kaylee shirked out of her mom's hold.

Ariana stepped farther inside, her boots squeaking on the tile. The air was cold but not freezing—someone had tried to keep heat running, but only just. Emergency lights glowed along the floor edges. A coffee cup sat on its side near a cluster of plastic chairs, contents long dried, staining the tile.

Lana drifted toward a bulletin board plastered with pamphlets. "This place doesn't feel abandoned. It feels like someone pressed pause."

Ariana understood exactly what she meant.

Reed circled slowly, his breath misting, and he pointed toward a gloomy hallway. "Power's out, but a generator's running. Though not well."

"How do you know that?" Damon asked.

Reed didn't miss a beat. "Truck stops have the same hum when backup units kick in." His eyes glinted strangely in the anemic light. "You learn to recognize the sound."

Eric nodded like he knew—or wanted everyone to think he did.

Wendy rubbed her arms briskly. "Let's find somewhere warm. A waiting area, or even a staff lounge. We can regroup, figure out rooms or something. We should stay close, but not necessarily together."

Kaylee rolled her eyes. "This is so creepy."

"She's not wrong." Damon said it lightly, but Ariana felt an undercurrent of low, coiled readiness. She stepped closer to him, linking their arms for her sake as much as his.

They moved deeper into the lobby as a loose cluster. A few chairs had toppled, one lying on its side as if somebody tripped or fled. Papers littered the floor near a nurses' station.

Ariana bent, picking it up. Discharge Summary dated four weeks ago. Barely a month.

She swallowed. "Someone was here recently. Very recently."

Lana hovered next to her, hugging her arms tight. "Do you think everyone evacuated? Maybe for the storm?"

"Storm hit fast," Reed said. "But hospitals don't empty without a reason."

Damon shot him a look. "And what reason would that be?"

Reed's mouth pulled into something like a smirk. "That's the question, isn't it?"

Wendy shifted, uncomfortable. "Let's keep moving. The storm's not letting up. We need to get warm."

The group moved toward the long corridor extending behind the lobby. The lights flickered in uneven intervals, leaving pockets of darkness that felt too deep, too watchful.

Ariana paused at the reception desk. The tan leather purse she'd noticed earlier was modern in design. It sat upright beside a contemporary jacket neatly folded over the chair. Not thrown, not dropped. Placed.

Someone intended to return.

Damon stepped beside her. "Ari?"

She showed him the purse wordlessly.

He exhaled through his nose. "Yeah. Someone left everything and walked away. Either willingly…" His jaw tightened. "…or not."

Their group had paused at the threshold of the hallway, the poor lighting stretching along the floor like a path into uncertainty.

Kaylee kicked the fallen coffee cup. "This sucks."

Reed stood at the front now, studying the building like he'd been here before. Or like he wished he hadn't.

Lana looked to Ariana, fear softening her voice. "We'll stay together, right? No one should wander alone."

Ariana nodded firmly. "We stick as a group."

Damon slid his arm around her waist protectively. "Agreed."

A gust of wind blasted against the windows behind them. The storm howled like something alive.

Ariana turned away from the entrance, forcing herself forward.

Whatever had happened here—whatever still lingered—they were inside now. And with the storm burying the cars and blocking the roads, they weren't getting out anytime soon.

All they could do was move deeper. And hope the hospital wasn't hiding something worse than the storm outside.

Chapter Five

Wendy didn't realize she was clenching her jaw until her teeth began to throb. She rubbed her aching temple, staring into the dreary hospital lobby while the storm hurled itself against the glass doors behind them.

The lights flickered, and Kaylee muttered something about horror movies.

It was all too much. The cold, the sopping clothes. Being stranded with strangers circling each other like nervous animals. And worst of all, the smell of antiseptic and dust and something else she couldn't name.

This was supposed to be their last good holiday as a family.

One final, picture-perfect Christmas before she slid the divorce papers across the dining room table in January and finally stopped pretending she could keep their life stitched together.

But of course Eric had been annoying her constantly on this trip. It seemed to be his hobby—see how long it takes to make Wendy snap and look crazy. He'd complained about the directions, harped on her about the overstuffed luggage, and criticized her for breathing too loudly in the car. She'd held herself together anyway. For Kaylee. For peace, or at least the illusion of something normal, even if it was only for one more season.

She'd been silently repeating a mantra to keep her cool. Once they got through the holidays, she would be able to start a life without Eric's constant bickering, grumbling, and demands. Even though she worked more hours than him and brought in more money, he still expected her to do all of the cooking, cleaning, and parenting. Meanwhile, he sat on the couch watching sports and barking orders.

It was all too much. She'd already put up with too many things for too long.

Now here they were, stranded in a blizzard, traipsing into an abandoned hospital like characters in the kind of scary movies she'd forbidden Kaylee to watch when she was younger. Now the teen read and watched whatever she wanted. Eric had told her—without asking Wendy's opinion—she could make her own decisions about her entertainment.

Wendy had tried to talk some sense into the man, but he painted her as the bad guy, and Kaylee wouldn't talk to her for two days. She and Eric were supposed to be a team, but he was more concerned with being king of the castle.

In a few weeks, she wouldn't have to deal with him any longer. No more criticisms of the way she cooked, cleaned, and parented. No more chainsaw-like snoring keeping her awake half the night. And best of all, no more man-child to have to pick up after and put up with. *That* would be the real vacation.

Then she could show Kaylee what a home without strife looked like. They would both be so much happier. Kaylee spent the majority of her time locked away in her room after arguing with Eric about boys. He might not care what she watched, but he insisted their daughter wouldn't date until she was thirty.

Once on their own, mother and daughter would be able to bond again, enjoy time together like they used to. Her heart warmed at the thought. In the meantime, she had to deal with Eric and this storm.

Eric stood off to the side, chatting with the gruff truck driver, Reed. Naturally. Eric always gravitated toward men who made him feel capable. Hunters, handymen. Loud, confident types. They talked in low tones, pointing down dark hallways as if they had any clue what they were doing.

Kaylee tugged her coat tighter, rolling her eyes at everything and everyone. Wendy reached out instinctively to tuck a strand of hair behind her ear before stopping herself. Kaylee barely allowed hugs these days, let alone motherly touches. She didn't want to push her away like Eric was doing so spectacularly.

Wendy's gaze drifted to Ariana. The young woman with a gentle presence somehow made even this nightmare feel steadier. Ariana carried herself with a confidence rarely seen in people so young. The way Damon hovered beside her, loving and concerned, made her heart ache for the marriage she always wanted but never got.

They looked like a team, true partners. That was what she *thought* she was getting when she married Eric. Prior to saying their vows, Eric had been the ideal man—always giving flowers, gifts, and compliments. Spouting off dreams and visions, when really it had all been a farce to get a ring on her finger so she'd be there to cook and clean for him.

He hadn't switched overnight. No, it had been slow. Barely imperceptible. Before she knew it, they had a baby and Wendy had all of the responsibility while Eric still had poker nights with his buddies and got to relax whenever he wanted. She barely got enough sleep, much less any down time.

Wendy hesitated. It didn't do any good to think about these things. Soon, it would all be behind her.

"Mom," Kaylee whispered, stepping closer. "Can we go home now?"

Wendy forced in a slow, measured, and steady breath. "As soon as we can, sweetheart."

Kaylee nodded, pressing herself closer without making a big deal of it.

Eric glanced over briefly, saw his daughter clinging to her, and his expression tightened with guilt. Or frustration. Or both. Wendy couldn't tell anymore. Nor did she care.

All she knew was this entire trip—this last chance to hold things together—was falling apart as wildly as their marriage.

Kaylee deserved better. They both did. And Wendy couldn't wait to give it to them.

The argument from earlier, the storm, the strangers, the eerie emptiness of this hospital... all pulsed under her skin, hot and jagged. She wasn't off-putting on purpose. If she was being honest with herself, she was terrified.

Terrified of failing Kaylee, terrified of what came next, and most of all, terrified the moment she let her guard down, everything would shatter.

Ariana approached then, gentle expression softening the sharp edges of Wendy's panic. "Are you holding up okay?"

Wendy startled, then straightened, gathering all her scattered pieces into something that looked composed. "I'm fine," she said quickly. Then she softened her tone. "Just... ready to get out of here."

Ariana nodded, her palm going to her stomach. "Me too."

She must be expecting. Hopefully she and Damon would be able to give their little one a better life than Wendy and Eric had managed. Guilt stung sharply. Oh, the things she would go back and change if she could.

For the first time since the storm started, Wendy felt the tiniest flicker of relief. Not safety—not even close—but the sense that she wasn't the only mother trying desperately to hold it together while the world crumbled around them.

A clang echoed from somewhere deep in the west wing.

Everyone froze. Wendy put a hand on Kaylee's arm. The fragile calm she clung to shattered like ice.

"Probably just a generator," Reed said.

"Yeah." Eric nodded, like he had any idea. Then he stood taller, obviously trying to impress Reed. "We should check it out."

Reed nodded in agreement. The others chimed in too.

Wendy held back a sigh.

Apparently they were all going deeper into the abandoned building.

Chapter Six

The hallway opened into a small waiting nook with half a dozen vinyl chairs, a vending machine humming as if on its last breath, and a TV mounted in the corner that flickered with static. The generator lights overhead buzzed in uneven pulses, casting shadows that moved when nothing else did.

Ariana pushed her gloves into her pockets, breathing in the faint scent of disinfectant mixed with cold air. The temperature was slightly warmer here, though not by much.

Wendy rubbed her hands together. "This is better, I think."

Kaylee slumped into a chair, crossing her arms dramatically. "Better than the car, at least."

Her father sat next to her and rubbed his temples.

Reed surveyed the room with a slow sweep of his eyes, lingering on the vending machine. "If this thing still works, we should grab what we can before the power dies."

Lana flinched. "You think it'll go out?"

"Storm like that?" Reed shrugged. "Wouldn't be surprised."

Damon bristled slightly, subtle but visible to Ariana. He

didn't like fear mongering—not in a building full of strangers and no way out. She gently touched his arm, grounding him before anything sharp could edge into his tone.

Wendy shuddered and glanced at her daughter. "Don't say that. We need to stay positive for Kaylee. She's just a kid."

Kaylee rolled her eyes. "I'm almost fifteen, and then I'll be learning to drive."

"The generators should hold." Damon glanced at the flickering lights. "But we have no idea how long they've been running already, so it would be wise to be ready for anything."

Ariana drifted toward the vending machine. A packet of peanut butter crackers sat crooked on its metal coil, as if someone had bought it but never retrieved it. Another tiny, quiet wrongness. "Anyone hungry?"

Kaylee didn't look up. "Is the Wi-Fi working in here?"

"There's no cell service." Wendy lowered herself into a chair next to her husband with a heavy sigh. "So probably not."

Kaylee groaned. "Great. This is barbaric."

Lana approached Ariana tentatively. "Are you okay? You seem… I don't know. Alert."

Ariana forced a smile. "Storms just make me nervous. And abandoned places."

Lana paled. "Same."

There was something vulnerable in other woman's eyes—raw edges, shadows, a flicker of something she wasn't saying. Ariana didn't press. She also didn't bring up any of her past experiences in similar circumstances. No matter how hard she and Damon tried to avoid trouble, it always seemed to be chasing after them.

As it seemed to be doing right then with this group of strangers in an abandoned hospital, of all places. She tried to stifle a shudder of her own.

Damon moved with purpose toward the nearby reception

alcove then flipped through a stack of scattered papers, his brows furrowed. "These are dated earlier this month."

Reed stepped closer. "Patient logs?"

"Supply lists," Damon answered. "Delivery confirmations. Someone worked here recently."

"Then where is everyone?" Reed's expression tightened, thoughtful in a way that again seemed just a little too informed. Or maybe Ariana was reading too much into it. He was a truck driver, after all. Deliveries would be his area of expertise.

Damon nodded at the older guy. "That's the question."

Wendy sat straighter, frowning at Reed. "Are you always this ominous? Because it's not helping."

Reed looked offended, though only mildly. "I'm realistic."

"You're being dramatic," Wendy said.

"Stop," Eric muttered.

His wife gave him an offended glance. "No. This situation is serious."

Eric crossed his arms. "Which is why we have to get along with everyone."

"What we need is—"

"Okay," Damon cut in, raising a hand. "Let's keep things simple. We'll stick together and find a warm room. Then we'll decide the safest place to wait out the storm."

Wendy exhaled, nodding.

Reed pressed his lips together but said nothing else.

Damon gravitated toward Ariana instinctively, protective and steady. "We should explore this wing since we know there's electricity."

Everyone gathered around them.

Lana drifted near Ariana, almost shadowing her.

Wendy hovered between concern and irritation, glued to her daughter's side. Eric stayed near them, but distanced.

Reed stayed just outside the circle, observant, rather than asking questions.

Ariana stepped around a small check-in counter, her boots squeaking softly. A jacket lay on the floor behind it—men's size, puffy. Not dusty. Recently worn. Maybe dropped in a rush.

She didn't mention it, but took note. Not because she wanted to hide anything, but because she didn't want to set the group off. Not when the atmosphere was already stretched tight like elastic.

Just like that, the overhead lights flickered out.

Everyone groaned or complained.

"We've got this." Damon turned on a wall-mounted flashlight from an emergency unit still holding charge. The beam sputtered then steadied, revealing a corridor sign.

Cafeteria →

Staff Break Room ←

Patient Rooms – East Wing ↓

"Break room," Wendy said. "Please. If there's a coffee pot, I might cry."

Kaylee groaned. "Can we at least look for a charger?"

"No outlets work when the grid's out," Eric said. "Generator only—"

"We get it," Wendy snapped.

Stress made people's patience short, and storms made them shorter. Tempers were likely to get worse with time, and cracks were already showing.

It was going to be a long night.

Ariana inched closer to Damon, who clicked the flashlight to a narrower beam and nodded toward the left hall. "Break room first. Then we can explore more."

Lana fell into step beside Ariana. "Thanks for being so calm," she whispered. "It helps."

Ariana wanted to tell her she didn't *feel* at all calm, that something inside her was prickling, a sense she'd learned never to ignore. But she only smiled reassuringly and squeezed Lana's arm.

Behind them, Reed muttered something to Eric—something Ariana couldn't quite catch.

Eric nodded slowly, as if they'd reached an unspoken agreement.

They all crept deeper into the hospital's corridors, footsteps echoing faintly. A wheeled cart stood abandoned near a doorway, stocked with fresh linens. A monitor blinked a soft green pulse in an empty room.

Someone had been here recently. Maybe still was. No, that couldn't be. The care workers wouldn't leave someone vulnerable behind.

Ariana didn't voice the worries. She just kept walking, one hand on her barely rounded belly, the other reaching for Damon.

Chapter Seven

The break room door stood slightly ajar, light leaking out in a thin, trembling line across the hallway floor. Damon paused first, lifting the flashlight toward the opening.

"Remind me," Wendy said, "why we're taking this creepy hall after we agreed to stay where there's electricity."

"Because you insisted on going to the break room," Eric muttered.

Damon nudged the door. It opened slightly. "There's light in here. Let's see if there is indeed a coffee pot."

Lana hovered closer to Ariana, and Kaylee inched in on her other side. The two didn't look at each other, but they seemed to reach the same silent conclusion. Ariana felt safe.

"Anyone hear anything?" Wendy whispered from behind them.

Ariana shook her head, but the air felt warm enough here that someone might have used this room recently. Heat lingered, even in a mostly powerless building.

Hide and Seek

Damon nudged the door with his foot. It swung fully open into a space that looked lived-in, not abandoned.

Ariana's pulse skipped. Both Lana and Kaylee stiffened next to her.

The break room was lit by a single buzzing fluorescent tube, flickering enough to make shadows jump along the walls. A table sat in the center, two chairs pulled out as though people had left mid-conversation. A thin, hospital-issued blanket was draped across one of the chairs. An open granola bar wrapper lay beside an empty foam cup.

Somebody had camped here. Recently.

Reed whistled low. "Looks like we're not the only ones using this hotel tonight."

"Not helping," Wendy snapped. "Can you just go five minutes without making everything worse?"

He held up his hands. "Just stating facts."

"Your facts are obnoxious," she shot back.

Eric muttered, "He's not wrong, Wen."

Wendy whirled on him. "Oh, perfect. Two doomsday prophets."

Eric exhaled hard, rubbing the bridge of his nose. "I'm not—"

Reed clapped him on the shoulder. "We're on the same page, buddy. That's all."

Ariana exchanged a look with Damon. That alliance was solidifying fast.

Kaylee rolled her eyes dramatically at the adults then leaned toward Ariana. "My mom's gonna combust if we're stuck here all night."

Lana whispered, "Mine would too."

Kaylee blinked. "You have a mom?"

Lana stiffened. "Everyone has a mom."

Kaylee muttered, "Not everyone."

A shame shadowed Lana's expression.

Ariana gently stepped between them, offering them both a small reassuring look. "Stress makes people say things they don't mean. Let's just take a breath."

They both nodded, breathing in sync with hers.

"You're so calm," Lana said. "Are you a therapist or something?"

"Sometimes it seems that way, given the people I work with, but no. However, my aunt is one, and I've picked up a lot from her."

"Can we focus?" Wendy stepped closer to her daughter, wrapping an arm around her.

Kaylee shrugged her off.

Damon stepped deeper into the room, running the flashlight slowly across the counters despite the flickering light overhead. "There's a half-full thermos here," he noted. "It isn't cold. Not exactly warm, either."

Ariana's stomach tightened. "Meaning whoever used it might not be far away."

Before anyone could respond, a soft shuffle sounded from the doorway behind them.

They all turned as one.

A woman stood there and gasped. She looked to be in her mid-fifties, and her skin was pale under the buzzing lights. Scrubs stuck out under a heavy cardigan, and her hair hung in tired gray curls around her face. She clutched a set of keys so tightly the metal pressed into her fingers. "I didn't expect anyone to be here."

Ariana stepped forward instinctively, hands raised in a gesture of calm. "We're stranded from the storm. It blocked the road and trapped our cars."

The woman's gaze darted from Damon to Reed to Eric, then to Wendy, Kaylee, and finally to Lana. She then turned her attention to Ariana. Something in her expression softened. "You're pregnant."

Ariana's protective instinct flared, and for some reason, her cheeks burned. She didn't respond. There was no way the woman could know. Ariana wasn't even showing yet. She'd only recently stopped wearing her tighter shirts.

The woman nodded, though Ari hadn't said a word. "You shouldn't be out in that storm. None of you should." She hesitated, then added, "My name's Marlene. I used to work here. Until it... shut down."

"Recently?" Eric asked.

Marlene's lips pressed into a tight line. "Recently enough."

Reed's eyes narrowed. "Why's the generator still running, then? And why's the break room warm?"

Marlene's fingers twitched at her keys. "Backup system. It kicks on automatically when the main power fails. It won't last forever, though."

"That doesn't explain the blanket." Wendy's voice was sharp. "Or the food."

Marlene didn't answer right away. Her gaze shifted to the granola wrapper, then to the not-cold thermos.

"I come by sometimes," she said finally. "Storms scare me. The roads aren't safe. I know this building better than I know my own home."

Ariana sensed truth in some of that, but not all.

Marlene's eyes darted too much. Her voice trembled—not from cold, but from something else. Fear? Guilt? Or awareness that she wasn't alone here either?

Damon stepped closer to Ariana. "Is anyone else here?"

Marlene hesitated for a beat too long. "No."

Reed snorted. "Convenient answer."

"That's enough," Damon warned him, voice low.

Reed bristled but didn't push back.

Marlene straightened, as if summoning old authority. "If you want shelter, you can stay. But some wings of the hospital are cold as a freezer. And others…" Her voice fell. "Others aren't safe to walk through in the dark."

"What does *that* mean?" Wendy demanded.

Kaylee shuddered. Lana stepped closer to her, their earlier awkwardness seemingly forgotten.

Ariana looked at the flickering fluorescent light, the open thermos, the blanket, the papers strewn in hallways, the purse at reception, the jacket behind the counter.

Something had happened here recently enough that the air still held warmth in pockets.

And someone else had been here. Maybe still was.

"All right," Ariana said softly, taking charge before anyone else could break into another argument. "We'll stay together. In this room for now. No one wanders off alone."

Damon nodded.

Lana and Kaylee moved closer to her.

Wendy sagged into a chair.

Eric and Reed shared a quiet, unreadable glance.

And Marlene watched them all with a tight, uneasy smile—the kind that tried to be welcoming but couldn't quite hide the dread beneath.

Ariana felt it again. A whisper of warning under her ribs.

They'd found shelter.

But safety was still far away.

Chapter Eight

The small room grew warmer once they all settled due to too many bodies in the cramped space. Someone had found a stack of disposable cups, and Marlene poured lukewarm water from the thermos into a few of them, passing them around with a trembling politeness.

Ariana accepted hers but didn't drink it. Something about the steam rising faintly from the cup made her stomach clench. Not nausea exactly, but a tightening, a pressure. Maybe a warning.

Damon sat beside her, knee touching hers, steady and solid. His presence alone helped keep her centered. Lana and Kaylee hovered close by the door, whispering in low bursts—bonding borne from shared fear more than anything else. Wendy argued with Eric about whether they should find actual beds, while Reed offered "practical advice" that only irritated Wendy more.

Marlene hovered near the counter, organizing and reorganizing items—stir sticks, a stack of napkins, sugar packets left over from who-knew-when—that didn't need touching.

Ariana's gaze drifted around the room again, taking in anachronistic elements for an abandoned space. A blanket draped over a chair. An open wrapper. A half-warm thermos. A rolling stool positioned near the window, as if someone had sat vigil there.

Nothing ominous, but every detail whispered that someone had been there. Very recently.

Her skin prickled with the awareness that Marlene wasn't telling the full truth about who that someone might be.

Wendy's voice rose behind her. "We can't just sit in this room all night. What if the generator fails?"

"Then we take turns watching it," Reed replied, calm in a way that made Ariana's nerves twitch.

"You're not in charge," Wendy snapped.

"Never said I was."

"Well you act like it."

Ariana tuned them out, her attention catching on something else. A faint, strange smell. Barely perceptible at first. It was just a whisper in the air, weaving between the scent of old coffee grounds and reheated plastic. She caught it in the back of her nose, a metallic sharpness tinged with something sickly sweet.

She inhaled again, slower. The scent tugged at some old, primal alarm deep in her memory.

A flash of cold concrete, a blindfold. Her own pulse thundering in her ears.

Whatever the odor was, it was wrong.

Ariana steadied a hand against the tabletop, the edge biting into her palm. "Does anyone smell that?"

Damon stopped mid-sentence, turning toward her with immediate concern. "Smell what?"

"That." Her breath tightened. "Something's off."

Wendy paused her argument long enough to sniff dramatically. "I don't smell anything."

Reed shook his head.

Eric shrugged.

Kaylee waved one hand. "Old building smell?"

Lana leaned in, brow furrowed. "Ariana? What does it smell like?"

Ariana opened her mouth, but the room tilted slightly, a wave of nausea rising suddenly and fiercely, as if her stomach had been waiting for an excuse to flip. She pressed a hand over her abdomen, breathing through her nose.

Damon was beside her instantly. "Ari? You look pale."

"I'm... I'm okay," she said, but the fib made her voice tremble. The smell still hovered, teasing her senses. "I just... I feel sick."

Kaylee wrinkled her nose. "Because of the smell?"

"No," Ariana whispered. "Because I am pregnant. Marlene was right." She threw the nurse a suspicious glance. "How'd you know?"

"After so many years in my line of work, I've learned to pick up on things. Things others miss, things I can't even explain with words."

Wendy softened, just for a second. Lana stepped closer, concern etching into her features. Even Reed's posture shifted, leaning subtly forward.

Marlene, though, went still. Her keys jingled faintly as her hand tightened around them.

"You shouldn't be breathing heavy air," the nurse said, voice thin. "This wing... it's colder because the vents still run. They draw in outside air. It's not harmful, but it's not ideal for someone in your condition."

Damon's jaw tightened. "Is that what we're smelling?"

Marlene hesitated just a fraction. "It's old machinery.

Nothing dangerous. You're all tired and wound up. Your mind fills in gaps."

The way she said it made Ariana's stomach twist even more.

Not because of defiance. She had no reason to distrust Marlene yet. But the nausea was real. Her first real pregnancy symptom hit like a punch.

Damon slid an arm around her waist. "Breathe. I've got you."

She leaned against him, the room settling back into focus.

Lana and Kaylee hovered at her side, quiet and looking worried.

Wendy pulled the blanket from the chair and handed it to Ariana without making eye contact.

Eric moved to help Reed inspect a cupboard, nodding in unspoken agreement as Reed pointed out the generator's hum.

"This is even more urgent than before." Wendy paced, muttering under her breath about emergency plans, then she stopped and stood guard beside Ariana.

Lana glanced around, expression nervous as a bird, ready to flutter at any movement.

Damon knelt in front of her, brows knitted with worry. "How bad is it?"

"It's okay," she said softly. "The smell just set it off."

But as she spoke, it came again, faint and drifting from somewhere deeper in the building. She turned her head toward the hallway.

And for the first time since entering the hospital, Ariana felt a single, terrifying certainty. Something—or someone—was out there.

She closed her eyes, pressing a hand protectively over her stomach.

They were not alone in this building.

Chapter Nine

Ariana's nausea hadn't fully passed, but the break room had settled into an uneasy rhythm. Shuffling bodies, whispered complaints, Wendy's pacing, and Reed and Eric murmuring in their quiet, suspicious partnership. Damon stayed close to Ariana, fingers brushing hers, anchoring her.

The strange smell still lingered, faint and drifting from the east wing. No one else noticed it—not even Damon. That alone made her feel more vulnerable than she wanted to admit.

She rose slowly, moving toward the doorway for a breath of cooler air. Lana followed her instantly. Kaylee, after a beat, drifted behind Lana, seemingly more annoyed by her parents than anything else.

Ariana inhaled deeply, the hallway's cold air easing her stomach. "Thanks for sticking close."

Kaylee shrugged. "It's creepy in there."

Lana nodded, arms wrapped around herself. "And everyone's arguing. I wanted a weekend alone but got this."

Ariana glanced back into the break room.

Wendy and Eric stood face to face now.

"You always do this," Wendy hissed. "You latch onto the first stranger who sounds decisive."

Eric's jaw tightened. "Reed is levelheaded."

"He seems *nosy*," Wendy snapped. "And why do you think he knows so much about backup power and old hospitals? He talks like he's been here before."

Eric hesitated a beat too long.

Reed folded his arms. "You're reaching. And if you'd listen, you might stay alive long enough for this storm to pass."

Wendy glared at him. "That sounds like a threat."

"I know about survival."

"It's just a storm. We'll be fine."

Damon rose as if ready to step in, but Ariana stepped back inside and touched his arm. This wasn't their argument.

A faint metallic clang echoed down the east wing corridor.

She froze.

Lana grabbed her sleeve.

Kaylee stiffened.

Damon turned, flashlight swinging toward the dark hallway.

Reed stopped mid-sentence, and Wendy too went silent.

Marlene stiffened, eyes darting to the corridor. "Probably... something falling. The vents shake loose sometimes."

But there was no airflow, no vent vibration. No reason for a metal door to move.

Eric took a step back. "Where's Kaylee?"

Kaylee scoffed. "I'm literally right here, Dad."

Eric exhaled shakily, hand sliding down his face. "I thought... never mind."

Reed gave a quiet, humorless chuckle. "Paranoia's contagious."

Another clang echoed, this one farther away. Deeper in the building.

Ariana's stomach dropped. "Someone should close the break room door."

Before anyone moved, Lana spoke. "Where's Marlene?"

Everyone glanced around.

Marlene wasn't anywhere in the room.

Wendy's eyes widened. "She was just here."

Eric cursed, and his wife nudged him.

Reed shook his head slowly. "I knew that woman was hiding something."

Damon turned the flashlight toward the hallway. "Marlene? If you're out here, say something."

Nothing.

Kaylee's voice broke thinly. "Did she go down the hallway? Why would she do that?"

Wendy shuddered. "This is exactly why we shouldn't trust anyone."

"Because yelling will help?" Eric shot back.

"Better than siding with strangers!"

Reed smirked. "You two should get couples therapy."

Wendy glared at him.

Ariana stepped into the hall, compelled by something she couldn't quite place.

Damon followed, his fingers grazing her elbow, grounding her but not pulling her back. "We should stay here with the group."

"I'm not going far." She didn't mean to separate from the others, but something flickered at the end of the corridor. A shadow, a shape. Perhaps a trick of the failing lights.

Or just Marlene. Either way, she had to know.

Ariana took two careful steps forward.

"Ariana?" Lana's soft whisper wavered behind her. "Should we get her?"

"No," Damon said. "Give her a second."

For a moment, everything held still.

Then a door creaked slowly, far down the east wing.

Ariana's breath hitched. She didn't move.

The sound grew louder, closer, like someone halfheartedly pushing open a heavy door... then letting it shut again.

It stopped as abruptly as it began.

And then footsteps. Measured and soft. Wrong.

Ariana's heartbeat thundered in her ears. She clutched her stomach.

Damon caught up with her, tensed beside her.

The footsteps came closer.

Marlene stepped into view. She appeared suddenly from a side hall, flustered but not frightened. "I... I'm sorry," she said, breath puffing in white clouds. "I went to check the other wings. I thought I heard something fall."

She didn't make eye contact with anyone.

Ariana felt it deep in her gut—Marlene wasn't telling the truth.

Reed appeared and shifted his stance. "Funny timing."

Marlene simply shrugged then bustled past them into the break room.

They followed her back to the small space.

Wendy glared at the nurse. "You scared us half to death!"

Marlene wrung her hands, voice cracking. "I didn't mean to. It's just this place... it has noises."

Ariana stared at her, trying to read the tremble in her voice.

Was it guilt? Fear? Or something else entirely?

The smell drifted again. It was fainter, but unmistakable now. A metallic sweetness.

Ariana swayed.

Damon caught her instantly. "Ari, hey breathe."

Lana moved to her other side. "You okay?"

She nodded shakily. "I can't deal with the smell."

Reed sniffed the air exaggeratedly. "I still don't smell anything."

"Because you aren't pregnant," Wendy quipped. "Pregnant women always smell things other people can't. I thought everyone knew that."

Reed scowled.

Marlene gave Wendy a knowing look. "Not all pregnant women have enhanced smell. No symptom is universal."

Eric squared his shoulders. "I have the olfactory glands of a trained K9, and I don't smell anything."

Wendy rolled her eyes.

"That doesn't mean it's not there," Ariana murmured.

Damon's grip tightened protectively. "We're not splitting up again. Especially not with that wing making noise."

Reed looked at Marlene. "What wing is that?"

Marlene swallowed. "East."

"Anyone staying there?" Reed pressed.

"No," Marlene said too quickly. "No one."

Ariana and Wendy shared a dubious glance. Neither of them believed Marlene.

Someone had been here and likely still was.

Whoever it was didn't want to be found.

And maybe Marlene didn't want anyone finding them either.

Chapter Ten

Wendy's entire body tensed as Eric and Reed stepped into the hallway to see if anything was out there. The echo of their footsteps trailed off into the kind of darkness that made her stomach twist. She hated every second of this but kept her mouth shut for Kaylee's sake.

For all their sakes.

The storm, the flickering lights, the noises. And now, the generator sputtering like the whole hospital was trying to take one final breath.

Wendy rubbed her arms hard, trying to banish the chill burrowing deep into her bones. She sank onto the edge of a chair, exhaling shakily. Kaylee hovered near the doorway for a moment, biting her lip the way she did when she was trying not to show fear.

"Come sit," Wendy urged softly, patting the chair beside her.

Kaylee hesitated. Then without even looking at her, she crossed the room and sat down next to Ariana.

Wendy froze.

Ariana immediately placed a soothing hand on Kaylee's back, murmuring something low and comforting. Kaylee leaned into her, shoulders curling inward, letting herself be comforted by someone who wasn't her mother.

The sight split Wendy clean down the middle. It was a mix of envy, sadness, and a sharp stab of something uglier.

Kaylee hadn't allowed Wendy to soothe her for months. Not since the arguments started piling up like unopened mail. Certainly not since Wendy's patience burned shorter, her nerves brittle from late nights and the looming secret of divorce papers hidden in her desk drawer at home.

She shoved down the ache. In all of her focus and anger toward Eric, she'd pushed Kaylee away. And she hadn't seen it until now.

Ariana's presence was caring, steady, and instinctive—everything Wendy used to be. Everything she'd been trying so hard to hold on to before life started fraying at the edges.

Kaylee whispered something to Ariana. Wendy leaned forward in spite of herself. She couldn't hear the words, but the tremulous vulnerability in her daughter's voice was clear. It was the tone she used when she needed safety.

And she hadn't chosen Wendy for it.

Heat rose up her throat. Shame, she realized. Humbling and painful.

She should be grateful Kaylee had someone to cling to right now.

This place was terrifying, the storm was unrelenting, and they weren't safe.

They weren't alone.

Of course Kaylee reached for the calmest person in the room.

But Wendy still found herself gripping the arm of her chair

hard enough to whiten her knuckles. She blinked rapidly, eyes burning.

"Mom?" Kaylee called suddenly, lifting her head.

The word hit her chest like a fist.

Wendy removed the expression from her face before Kaylee could read it. "Yeah, sweetheart?"

Kaylee didn't move from Ariana's side. She didn't crawl into Wendy's arms or reach for her hand. But she offered a small, uncertain glance. It was a truce of sorts. "Are you okay?"

Wendy hesitated. "I'm fine, honey. Just tired."

Ariana looked up at Wendy then, eyes soft, understanding too much.

Wendy forced a small, brittle smile and nodded toward Ariana. "She's in good hands."

Ariana shook her head gently, not rejecting the comment but rejecting the distance. "She's scared. That's all. She needs all of us."

Wendy's throat tightened. She nodded and sank back into her chair, hugging her arms around herself.

She couldn't fall apart now. Not in front of Kaylee, not when everything was unraveling so quickly. Besides, Eric would return soon, and she couldn't let him see any weakness in her.

This holiday was supposed to be their last peaceful one together.

Instead, it was turning into a nightmare she couldn't wake from.

And her proud, stubborn, hurting daughter was finding comfort in someone else's arms. Kaylee didn't leave Ariana's side. Not for a second. Every time Wendy tried to move closer, Kaylee instinctively shifted back toward Ariana, like the girl had found a safer orbit and wasn't ready to leave it.

It stung more than Wendy wanted to admit.

Ariana winced suddenly, hand pressing low on her abdomen. "Sorry, uh, I need to find a restroom."

Wendy forced a smile, mother-to-mother. "Of course you do. Let's see if one of these halls still has running water."

But when she led the way toward the nearest restroom sign, the corridor felt colder than before. Darker. Like the storm had seeped into the walls themselves.

Ariana paused at the entrance. "Can you two wait here? I'll just be a minute."

"Sure." Kaylee nodded reluctantly.

Wendy stood with her back straight, arms folded, scanning the hallway because someone had to. Every distant clang made her flinch. Somewhere deeper in the building, a door creaked on its hinges. Pipes that sounded like footsteps shifted in the dark.

A quiet thud echoed from inside the restroom.

Wendy tensed. "Ariana?"

Ariana's voice floated back, thin but steady. "I'm fine. Just a stall door sticking."

But Wendy didn't miss the tremble in her tone.

Or the second sound—soft, almost like a whisper—farther back.

Kaylee pressed closer to Wendy, eyes wide. "Did you hear that?"

"I'm sure it was just the wind," Wendy fibbed, fingertips going numb.

Ariana emerged moments later, pale but trying to smile. "Sorry. Everything's a chore right now."

Kaylee slid back into her side immediately, relief lighting her face in a way that clenched something deep in Wendy's chest.

Wendy closed her eyes for a moment, steadying her breath.

She would hold herself together. Even if it hurt, and even if she had to break quietly later.

For Kaylee, she would stay strong.

No matter how hard it was. They were going to get through this nightmare, and would soon start over with a new home and a fresh chance at a restored relationship.

They just had to get through the night.

Chapter Eleven

Ariana steadied herself against the wall, the last of the nausea fading like a dimming light. Damon stayed close, hand on her back.

Lana and Kaylee hovered nearby, appearing wary now that everything felt wrong.

Marlene's return had left everyone looking more jostled than before. Reed watched her like a puzzle he was determined to solve. Eric stayed close to him, arms folded.

Wendy glared at both men as if their very existence offended her. But when her gaze slid to Ariana, her hard expression softened, and her shoulders lowered a fraction. She made her way over to Ari. "You shouldn't be standing in cold hallways." Her tone was gentler than she'd used so far. "'Morning' sickness is no joke, storm or no storm."

Ariana blinked, surprised by her warmth. "I'm okay. Really."

Wendy stepped closer, lowering her voice. "How far along?"

"Almost twelve weeks."

Wendy's features softened in a way Ariana didn't expect. "That was the worst stretch for me with Kaylee. All smells made me sick. Even the detergent in our sheets. I swear everything sent me running for the porcelain throne."

Kaylee groaned loudly. "Mom, really?"

Wendy shot her daughter a look, but it held more affection than annoyance. "I'm just saying I get it. It's a weird kind of misery. You'll understand one day, and then we'll commiserate together."

The teen blanched.

"She's right," Ariana admitted, feeling a small smile tug at her lips despite the situation. "But it's worth it."

Wendy nodded, something vulnerable flickering across her face. "Always."

Damon squeezed Ari's hand.

Reed's voice cut through the softer moment like a blade. "So, what's the plan? Sit here until the storm passes? Listen to ghosts rattle vents? Wait for the power to cut and freeze to death?"

Eric nodded, backing him up. "We should at least explore the west wing. Might be warmer."

Wendy's protection evaporated. "Absolutely not. We're not wandering into another dark hallway. Not with a teenager and a pregnant woman."

Reed smirked. "Are you scared?"

Eric stepped closer to his wife and shot the other man a look. "Hey."

Wendy didn't seem to notice, her gaze fixed on the trucker. "Scared of what? You? Maybe I should be, but I'm not."

"Okay." Damon's tone was sharp as he stepped between them before the argument blew up. "We're not separating. Not until we know more about this place."

"Might be a good idea." Reed lifted his chin. "Us men can handle ourselves."

Wendy rolled her eyes but didn't say anything.

Marlene cleared her throat, drawing all attention again. Her hands twisted around her keyring, the metal clinking softly. "The west wing is administrative, mostly offices and storage. If you must explore, start there. It's safer."

Reed narrowed his eyes. "How do *you* know it's safe?"

"Because I *worked* here. I know all the wings."

"Funny," Reed countered, "you didn't know we were right behind you when you wandered off a minute ago."

Marlene's face went rigid, her jaw trembling. "I wasn't... Like I told you, I heard something fall. I went to check it out."

"Did you see anything?" Ariana asked gently.

Marlene's gaze flicked quickly toward the east hall. "No."

"Liar," Reed muttered.

They stared each other down.

Eric cleared his throat. "We're all on the same team. And we'll need to stay that way if we want to stay alive."

Wendy stared at her husband. "What is it with you two and your 'staying alive through the night' narrative? It's just a storm."

The smell Ariana had noticed earlier drifted again, faint but sharp, brushing her senses and making her stomach clench.

Damon wrapped his arm around her shoulders, pulling her close.

Wendy noticed. "Really, Ariana, you should sit down. You look exhausted."

"I'm fine." The truth was a different thing entirely. Her instincts were buzzing now, louder than the hum of the generator, and louder than Reed's arrogant muttering.

Someone else was in this building. And Marlene seemed to know enough to fear that person.

A soft metallic click echoed down the east wing hallway, unmistakable and out of place. Everyone fell silent.

Reed's gaze darted all around. "*That* wasn't the vents."

Eric glanced around. "Someone else is here."

"You said this place was empty." Fear colored Kaylee's tone as she glared at Marlene. She inched away until her back was pressed against the wall.

Marlene's mouth opened then closed. Because she had no answer. At least not one she was going to voice.

Damon squeezed Ariana's fingers.

Lana edged closer again, her voice a whisper.

Before Ariana could say anything, Wendy touched her arm. It was a brief, surprising gesture of solidarity.

"We'll stick close," Wendy said softly. "Especially to you."

Ariana met her gaze. Wendy's eyes were tired, stubborn, and fierce. She had the look of someone who'd do anything for her child, even snap at strangers and fight storms. Mother to mother. A fragile, important alliance forming in real time.

Damon's hand tightened on Ariana's waist. "We'll all head back to the break room, and then decide our next move."

Behind them, the east hall whispered again. It was a faint shuffle, barely audible but undeniably real.

Ariana didn't look back. She didn't need to.

Because it was obvious someone was there.

Chapter Twelve

The group trudged back to the break room in a tight cluster, all footsteps echoing in the cold corridor. The glow from the single flickering light above the door cast a jittery pattern along the walls, making their shadows ripple ahead of them.

Ariana's stomach had settled mostly, but her senses were still rattled—not just from the smell, but from the sharp click of that distant door. She wasn't imagining things. As soon as they stepped back into the room, she felt a small shift.

Damon noticed too. His hand curled instinctively around hers. "Something's different."

Wendy stepped in past them and froze. "Wait. Was that chair like that before?"

One of the chairs at the table had been previously pushed in but was now pulled out an inch or two, angled slightly toward the door. Not dramatic or overtly obvious. But moved.

Kaylee frowned. "Maybe someone bumped it?"

Wendy moved closer to her daughter. "No one was behind us. Nobody touched anything."

Eric scanned the room, brows furrowing. "Maybe the floor isn't level."

Reed snorted. "Yeah, because chairs drag themselves."

Lana wrapped her arms around herself. "I don't like this place anymore."

Neither did Ariana. The room felt tighter now, as if the air had shifted from merely cold to watchful.

"We should sit." Wendy rubbed her temples. "I'm done walking for a while."

Surprisingly, she moved toward Ariana, hovering. "Let's all rest for a few minutes. Let our nerves settle."

Ariana nodded, lowering herself into one of the chairs. Damon stood behind her, one hand on the chair and the other on her shoulder.

Reed and Eric whispered with low, determined energy, glancing between the hallway and the room. Plotting something.

Ariana bristled. "Anything you want to share with the class?"

Reed broke away from the murmured conversation. "Storm's not going anywhere, and something's off in this place. We should check the rest of the wing. Might be able to find something useful, like keys or emergency gear."

Eric nodded. "The two of us will be able to move faster without everyone crammed together."

Wendy stiffened. "So you're just leaving? Great."

Eric sighed. "We're not leaving. We're checking the area. It's fine, Wendy."

Ariana turned and gave Damon a concerned glance.

He gave a slight nod, acknowledging her worry.

Wendy frowned. "I don't like this."

Reed shrugged as if the point were settled. "Eric and I will go. The rest of you can stay."

Ariana felt Damon tense behind her. "You don't get to decide that."

Reed smiled in a tight, needling way. "Didn't say I did. Just seems practical."

Damon stepped closer. "We're not splitting up unless we all agree on it."

Kaylee muttered, "He's gonna punch Reed."

Lana shook her head. "He won't."

Damon cleared his throat. "I'm not hitting anyone, but I am going with you."

"Fine." Reed frowned, but didn't argue. "Women stay, rest, keep warm. Simple."

Wendy placed a gentle hand on Ariana's shoulder. "It's for the best." Her tone shifted again into mother-to-mother solidarity. "You shouldn't be walking around, or breathing strange smells. And honestly... after what just happened, I'd rather stay put with you than chase shadows down another hallway."

Ariana touched her arm, grateful. "I appreciate that."

Damon looked torn between protective instincts warring with pragmatism. "Ari, are you going to be okay?"

"You won't be far." Her pulse fluttered nervously. "And we have strength in numbers."

Marlene stood by the counter again, staring at the moved chair with a rigid expression she quickly masked when she felt Ariana's gaze. "I'm stronger than the three of you men. I can protect these ladies."

Somehow, Ari didn't doubt that. But she herself also taught women's self-defense courses, so pregnant or not, she wasn't helpless.

Reed slapped Eric's shoulder. "Let's go before the generator dies."

Damon hesitated one more beat, cupping Ariana's cheek. "Call out if anything feels wrong."

She managed a small smile. "Will do."

He kissed her forehead then straightened, posture tense and ready.

Reed and Eric were already heading for the hallway. Damon joined them, flashlight raised.

The moment the men stepped out, their absence made the room's atmosphere shift.

Kaylee slid her chair closer to hers, trying to look cool but failing miserably.

Lana sat beside her, biting her lip. Wendy perched between them all, shoulders tight but gaze steady.

Marlene lingered in the doorway, listening to the retreating footsteps with a strange expression of mixed relief and fear.

Ariana inhaled slowly. The odor brushed her senses again, but she didn't say anything.

The storm outside howled. A door clicked somewhere deep in the hospital.

Must be the men.

Someone might be walking toward them too. She bristled at the thought.

But Damon was as well versed in self-defense moves as she was. They both taught the classes.

Hopefully Reed and Eric were actually trustworthy.

She'd be ready to run if she heard any screams.

Chapter Thirteen

The silence practically screamed after the men left. It was quiet in a way that didn't comfort. The generator hummed weakly overhead, its steady thrum broken by the occasional threatening sputter. Snow lashed against the high windows like something trying to claw its way in.

Ariana sat with her hands folded over her stomach, taking slow, even breaths. Wendy perched beside her, rubbing her palms together for warmth. Lana and Kaylee sat cross-legged on the floor near their knees, whispering about nothing important—anything to distract themselves from being stranded in an enormous building with strangers.

Marlene lingered near the counter, flipping through a magazine. She kept her back partially to them, her shoulders tense, posture rigid.

Ariana studied her but couldn't pick up on anything in particular.

"They shouldn't go into the west storage hall." Marlene's outburst after such a long period of quiet was jarring.

The room went still.

Wendy frowned. "Why not? What's wrong with it?"

Marlene blinked, as if surprised she'd said anything at all. Her fingers trembled on the cracked plastic of a sugar packet.

"I mean, the floor is uneven. There are... things stored there that could fall."

Kaylee raised a brow. "That sounds like a lie."

Wendy flicked a quick glance at her.

"It wasn't," Marlene insisted.

Ariana caught her gaze. "How long did you work here before the shutdown?"

"Long enough."

Lana hugged her knees. "Then you know why it closed."

Marlene's eyes shifted. "Some facilities shut down for budget reasons. Or... because they become unsafe for patients."

The air shifted, and Ariana sat up straighter. "Unsafe how?"

Marlene pressed her lips together. "I don't know."

Wendy leaned in, irritation evident in her eyes. "Marlene, if there's something we should know, just spit it out."

A clatter echoed from the hallway.

Kaylee yelped. Lana grabbed her arm. Wendy bolted upright.

Ariana froze.

It wasn't a chair or a vending machine coil or a vent. No, it was something heavy.

Something falling.

Or someone.

Marlene stepped back from the door, face paling. "The storm. That's all. Wind pushes debris."

"That wasn't debris," Wendy said. "That was *inside*."

There was no denying the fact because they'd all heard it. All jolted at the same instant.

For a tense moment, no one moved.

Then slowly, they settled again. If not comfortably, at least collectively. Lana and Kaylee huddled closer to Ariana and Wendy. Marlene straightened her cardigan, staring at the door with a haunted expression. She played with the magazine.

Ariana's instincts screamed at her that nothing about this was over. But she forced her breathing rate to remain steady.

For a few seconds, everything quieted.

Then a scream fractured the silence. A man's. Raw, terrified.

Echoing from the hallway.

The direction Damon and the other men had gone.

Blood drained from Ariana's body.

Kaylee covered her mouth. Lana gasped. Wendy leapt to her feet.

Ariana's heart hammered against her ribs, and she rose, shoving the chair behind her. She had to get to Damon.

Wendy grabbed her arm. "Ariana, don't—"

Ariana ran. Straight into the hall, adrenaline overriding instinct, Damon's name on her lips.

Footsteps and clipped words followed her, but Ariana didn't glance back. Her focus was on Damon.

The hallway stretched long, generator lights buzzing and flickering. Ariana's pulse pounded, drowning out other noises.

Another shout broke through. Closer now. Reed's voice this time.

Eric yelled for help.

Damon. She needed to see Damon.

They reached the west wing doorway as the men appeared around the corner. Damon first, flashlight trembling in his grip, eyes wide and shocked. Reed and Eric were behind him, both pale, both shaken.

"Stay back!" Damon held out a palm.

Ariana froze in place. "What happened?"

Reed's voice cracked. "We found someone."

Eric gasped for air. "A body."

The cold air shifted.

Terror snaked down Ari's spine. "Someone the hospital staff left behind?"

Damon didn't answer. His jaw clenched in a way that told her everything she needed to know.

This body wasn't old.

It was fresh.

Reed scrubbed a hand over his face. "It's not from the storm. It... it wasn't an accident."

Wendy gasped, pulling Kaylee against her.

Lana covered her mouth, eyes wide.

Ariana felt her knees weaken. Damon caught her instantly.

Marlene pressed a fist to her lips, whispering something unintelligible—maybe a prayer, maybe something else altogether.

The hallway fell into a terrible, unnatural silence.

Someone had died here. Recently. Within hours, maybe minutes.

Since they'd arrived.

Whoever was in this building, they weren't only capable of murder.

They'd already committed it.

Chapter Fourteen

They hurried back to the break room in a stumbling cluster of boots slapping tile and sharp breaths. The hallway echoed with the sounds of fear. Ariana clutched Damon's sleeve the whole way, feeling him tremble beneath the layers of his jacket.

Wendy and Kaylee moved as a single unit, arms tangled. Lana hovered close to Ariana again, eyes red and wide, breathing shallow like she might faint. Reed muttered curses under his breath. Eric's face had gone gray, jaw clenched so tight Ariana could almost hear it creak.

But Marlene... she strode at a normal pace as if they hadn't just found someone murdered. How could she be so composed after seeing that?

As soon as they reached the break room, Wendy exploded. "What the hell was that? A body? Someone died in this place—and not from natural causes or a botched surgery!"

Reed threw an accusing look at Marlene. "You knew something was off. You walked right into the dark earlier, and now you're barely fazed."

Marlene flinched but didn't deny anything. "I told you the wing wasn't safe."

"That's not the same as warning us there might be a murderer." Wendy paced furiously.

Kaylee slunk into a chair, shaking. Lana slid down next to her and grabbed her hand.

Eric leaned against the wall, rubbing his face. "This place is a nightmare. I knew we should've left earlier. We'd have missed all of this and been at our hotel right now."

Wendy glared at him.

Reed tugged on his shirt. "Someone's here. Someone who left a fresh body in a freaking office."

Marlene stiffened but said nothing.

Ariana wrapped her arms around herself. The smell from earlier was somehow stronger now, impossible to ignore. And every time she breathed in, her stomach roiled.

Damon stayed quiet next to her, not even offering comfort. Didn't even look at anyone else, just stared at the floor, knuckles white around the flashlight.

Ariana moved toward him slowly, gently touching his arm. "Damon?"

No response.

She tugged lightly. "Look at me."

Finally, he raised his eyes. The devastation in them punched the air from her lungs. "Can we talk?" he whispered. "Alone."

She pulled him into the hall, stepping just outside the break room doorway. They were still visible and close but kept enough distance from the others to speak without them hearing.

Damon leaned against the wall, the flashlight trembling in his hand. His breathing was uneven, almost ragged. "It wasn't just a murder… it was…"

Her breath hitched. "What?"

"Staged."

Ariana's skin prickled. "How?"

His jaw twitched. "The position of the body. The... the scene. He was lying on his back with his arms straight out. Shoes missing. Face turned to the wall." Damon's voice broke. "That's exactly how my father left his third victim."

Ariana felt cold all the way through. "It has to be a coincidence."

He shook his head, pacing in a short, frantic line. "It's... Ari, it's exactly the same. Not similar. Just like the pictures."

"You've been looking at pictures?"

Damon looked away. "I had to know what he'd done."

"He didn't do this." She stepped in front of him, placing her hands on his chest. "Your father is dead. He's not here."

"I know," he whispered, pressing his forehead against hers. "Obviously he didn't kill the person in that office, but someone did. They know who I am, who *he* was, and they're sending me a message."

She shook her head. "That's not possible."

"Isn't it? How hard would it be for someone to put the pieces together?"

"But they couldn't know you'd be here."

"That's just it." Damon's voice shook. "They do. Someone knows exactly how my father killed and is recreating it down to the smallest detail. And they want me to know."

Ariana's heart pounded loudly in her ears. "But... nobody could guess you're related to Cal Jones. It's one of the most common last names around. People don't hear 'Jones' and think of him."

"Someone obviously figured it out—and they've made it more than clear."

"That's a drastic way to get the point across."

"I doubt *this* was the point. This was just a message."

His words took her breath away for a moment. "What's the point?"

He didn't answer. He didn't have to.

The truth shimmered in the air between them, dark and terrible.

Someone knew Damon's secret and had targeted him. Worse, they'd managed to trap them here. The detour, the collapsed bridge... It was an outlandish and meticulous plan.

The kind made by a keen, deranged mind.

Damon cupped her cheek with shaking fingers. "Ari... if they know I'm Cal's son, what else do they know?"

Ariana pressed her hand over his, steadying him. "We'll figure it out. This isn't him. It's someone trying to frighten you. None of the people who worked with him were really that smart. They just followed orders, remember? They'll mess up, and we'll find them."

"And then what? Kill them? Get ourselves killed? There's no way I'm going to let anything happen to you." A fire lit in his eyes.

"Nobody else is dying."

"Then what will we do if we find the person?" Damon looked around, his nostrils flaring.

Ariana started to respond, but behind them, Wendy's voice rose again in panic. Kaylee cried softly, while Reed and Eric argued in harsh whispers. Marlene didn't make a peep.

Ariana kept her gaze locked on Damon. "I won't let them hurt you."

"It isn't me I'm worried about." His voice was practically a growl.

"Look at me." She guided his chin until their gazes met. "We train people in self-defense. If anyone is capable of knocking them down and restraining them, it's us."

But even as she said it, the metallic smell curled through the hallway again. It reminded her that she was more vulnerable than she wanted to admit, though she would protect their baby... no matter the cost.

The killing wasn't just a reenactment, it was clearly a message. To Damon and probably her too.

Someone in this hospital was playing a game and had just made the first move.

She and Damon would have to find the advantage so they could make the final play.

Chapter Fifteen

Wendy stood near the doorway under the pretense of needing air. Not that there was a hint of fresh anything in this place. Just cold, stale hospital breath drifting through the hall. She crossed her arms tightly, pretending she wasn't listening.

Reed and Eric, a few feet away in the shadowed corner, didn't notice her. They were too absorbed in their low, urgent whispers. Eric never noticed her when he was with another man.

"I'm telling you," Reed said, voice pitched low but forceful. "She's hiding something."

Eric rubbed his forehead. "Marlene's just scared. You can't blame her—even Damon was freaked out by the body."

Reed snorted softly. "That woman didn't so much as blink at seeing the scene. Didn't flinch when the lights went out. And she keeps looking down the east wing like she expects someone to walk out of it."

Eric hesitated. "She's a nurse. Probably sees death every week."

"Murdered ones?"

Wendy felt a cold twinge behind her ribs.

Eric didn't respond to Reed's question.

"She's the only one who knows this hospital," Reed continued. "She knows the layout. Knows where things are, where people could hide."

"Or where people could die," Eric said.

A beat of silence.

Wendy's pulse hammered. She held her breath, trying to calm it and hear better.

Reed leaned closer. "Think about it. Why was she here when the storm hit? Why alone? Why does she have keys?"

Eric didn't answer right away. "She could trap us anywhere. The main doors could be locked now for all we know."

Wendy's stomach dropped. He wasn't wrong, as much as she hated admitting it.

Reed exhaled in a low growl. "We need to keep an eye on her."

Something clattered deeper in the hospital, perhaps a tray. Another metallic echo bouncing along the walls.

Eric stiffened.

Reed turned sharply toward the sound.

Wendy stepped back fast, pretending she hadn't heard anything when they turned around. She rejoined the group, smoothing her hair even though her hands shook.

Marlene stood by the counter as always, stiff and fidgeting. Her fingers wrapped around her keyring like she meant to anchor herself. Perhaps defend herself.

Kaylee and Lana huddled closer to Ariana.

Ariana leaned into Damon, and his arm cinched around her protectively.

Wendy rubbed her arms, the hush in the room making her

chest tight. She glanced at Ariana, wanting to drift toward her, maybe confide something, anything.

Ariana had a steadiness that Wendy craved like a lifeline. Mother to mother.

But Ariana was pressed close to Damon, their heads almost touching as they murmured to each other. A sealed unit. A wall Wendy didn't dare approach.

She swallowed around the lump in her throat. If her husband wasn't so selfish, they could've had a bond like that. But he preferred a servant to a partner. Little did he know his days of receiving her free labor were numbered.

Later, when things calmed down, she would try talking to Ariana. The younger woman might have some insight as to how Wendy could reach Kaylee. When Ariana wasn't wrapped in Damon's arms like the world was ending, and when Wendy didn't feel like the intrusive outsider in every corner of her own life.

For now, she stayed where she was, arms wrapped around herself, mind spinning with Reed's warnings, ears tuned for more whispers behind walls.

And as she watched, Marlene turned her head sharply toward the east wing again. It was like she heard something the rest of them didn't.

A cold, creeping certainty slid under Wendy's skin.

Reed might be right.

Something was very wrong with Marlene.

And Wendy wasn't going to ignore it.

She couldn't afford to. Not with Kaylee here.

Wendy would do whatever it took to protect her daughter—even if nobody here would protect her. Her own husband surely wouldn't. Why would he start now?

Another clatter sounded out in the hallway. Louder than before.

Hide and Seek

The group was definitely not alone.

Chapter Sixteen

Ariana's stomach churned acid, but she did her best to ignore it. The break room felt smaller and even more cramped by the minute. After Damon's confession, Ariana stayed close to him, her shoulder pressed to his as the group argued, paced, or clung to each other in silence.

Patience and alliances both were wearing thin, and the fear previously binding them together wasn't quiet anymore.

Reed paced the length of the room for what had to be the tenth time in under a minute, muttering under his breath. Eric watched the door like he expected something to step through it at any moment. Wendy sat rigid beside Ariana, fingers drumming a frantic rhythm against her knee. Kaylee and Lana sat curled up on the floor again, sticking close to Ariana and Wendy.

Marlene, however, hovered near the counter, her expression tight and unreadable.

Reed finally spun around. "We need to talk about why we're all here. Because someone did that intentionally. It was no accident, and someone left it there for us to find."

Wendy scoffed. "For *us* to find? We can't know their intentions."

"No? Look around. Storm hits the exact moment we're on this mountain? Bridge washes out? Cell towers drop? Murder scene staged in the hospital we all just happen to stumble into? Seems pretty suspicious."

Ariana and Damon exchanged a quick look before turning back to the others.

Eric nodded, jaw clenched. "He's right. It's not coincidence."

Damon's arm curled around Ariana's shoulders, pulling her closer. His grip had grown firmer by the minute, as if a claim, a shield, a barrier.

She didn't push him off, but the tension buzzing through him was undeniable.

Reed pointed at Eric. "You were headed west. Why?"

Eric frowned. "Family gathering."

"Obviously," Wendy muttered.

"In the middle of a blizzard?" Reed challenged.

Eric's jaw tightened. "I didn't check the forecast."

Wendy crossed her arms. "Because he never checks anything."

Eric shot her a look but said nothing.

Reed turned next to Lana. "What about you? A young woman driving alone into the mountains?"

Lana stiffened. "I'm just taking a weekend to myself." Her voice cracked. "Or at least I was."

Kaylee studied her new friend. "You don't have luggage."

Lana's gaze snapped to the floor. "I packed light. It wasn't like I was going to be gone for a week."

Ariana wanted to comfort her, because Lana's expression of worry ran deep. She could be fleeing something or someone. Running fast, running scared.

She knew that feeling all too well. Some memories never really faded. They just got pushed back until they returned to the surface.

Reed moved on, eyes narrowing at Marlene. "And what about you? You 'hang out' in abandoned hospitals for fun? Seems more like a teenage hobby than one for someone your age."

Marlene's fingers tightened around her keyring. "I told you, I live down the ridge and come here sometimes during storms. It's comforting. Not that I need to explain myself to you."

"That's not normal," Wendy mumbled.

Marlene glared at her. "Neither is finding a dead body in a closed facility."

Silence crashed over the room, heavy and suffocating.

Reed finally turned toward Damon. "And you two? Why are you here?"

Ariana's pulse spiked.

Damon's hand tightened on her shoulder. "We're visiting family," he said evenly. "And taking a couple days for ourselves first."

Reed's gaze sharpened. "You're pale as hell. You looked like you were going to pass out when we found that body."

"Did you expect me to dance around?" Damon stared him down. "That's a normal response to stumbling on a murder scene."

"We all saw the body," Reed said. "But you—"

"Enough," Ariana cut in. "This whole situation was unnerving before. Now it's on steroids."

Lana nodded firmly, and Kaylee followed suit. Even Wendy moved closer to Ariana's side.

Alliances were shifting again.

Reed scoffed but backed off.

For a moment, the only sound was the generator whirring.

Click.

The lights went out. Pitch black engulfed the room. The generator's hum sputtered, coughed, then died completely.

Someone gasped. Somebody else cursed.

A chair toppled over.

Ariana grabbed Damon's arm, her heart pounding against her ribs. "Damon—"

"I'm here." He pulled her closer. "I've got you."

A mechanical clunk echoed from the hallway outside. It was the heavy, unmistakable sound of a door locking.

"What was that?" Wendy whispered, voice rising in panic.

"Back door," Marlene said. "Sometimes it auto-locks when power shuts off."

"No," Damon snapped. "Someone is locking us in."

Metal scraped against metal. Another door. Then another.

The building was shutting itself down. Or worse, someone was shutting it down.

Kaylee whimpered. Lana wrapped an arm around her.

Movement sounded as people shuffled around.

Ariana's breath came faster, trembling. Damon's arms tightened, his protectiveness turning almost into a near chokehold.

"Damon," she whispered. "You're squeezing me."

He loosened but didn't let go. "Sorry. I just... I can't let anything happen to you."

Reed's voice cut through the darkness. "Hey! Flashlights! Phones!"

Damon clicked on the flashlight he still held, casting a narrow beam across the room. Faces emerged from the dark like ghosts—pale, frightened, drawn.

Ariana reached for her phone, hope flickering. But it was dead. She had planned on charging it once they settled into their hotel room. If she'd known they'd end up here, she'd have charged it during the drive.

Others muttered about having no power on theirs.

Wendy tried hers. A faint light flickered before the screen darkened.

Marlene stood nearest the door, keys trembling in her hand.

"Why are you over there?" Reed scowled at her.

Marlene didn't answer.

A soft sound floated down the hallway.

Not mechanical this time.

A whisper, a voice. Human.

Every hair on Ariana's arms rose.

Lana whimpered. Wendy's hand found Ariana's arm and held on.

The whisper came again. Closer now, just beyond the doorway.

Damon lifted the flashlight, shielding Ariana with his body. "If anyone comes through that door," he growled, voice low and dangerous, "they go through me first."

Tension choked the room with fear and paranoia. Damon's fierce protectiveness threatened to ignite into something volatile.

Ariana gripped his wrist. "It's okay. We're here, and we're together."

But even as she said it, the whisper echoed again.

If there was any doubt about them being alone, it was gone now.

Someone else was out there.

And they were a killer.

Chapter Seventeen

The unmistakably human whisper from in the hallway still lingered in Ariana's ears, and Damon's arm locked protectively around her waist. His body coiled like a spring, ready to shield, ready to break if anyone touched her.

Everyone seemed to feel the shift. The invisible line drawn through the break room, splitting it into islands. The walls felt like they were closing in with every passing second.

Kaylee scooted closer to Ariana's leg, not looking toward the doorway.

Wendy hovered behind them, trembling but squaring her shoulders.

Reed and Eric stayed pressed together near the table like a single unit, both gripping their useless phones like makeshift weapons. Their eyes flicked constantly to the door and then to Marlene.

Always to Marlene.

She stood unmoving by the counter, keyring glinting in the narrow beam of the flashlight.

"You heard those doors lock, right?" Reed snapped. "That wasn't wind or a power surge—that was someone using a key."

Eric's turned to Marlene. "Which she has."

She stiffened. "These keys are for emergency access, nothing else."

"You sure?"

"Yes." Marlene's face tightened

Kaylee clutched Ariana.

Damon's grip on her waist tightened protectively.

The air between Reed and Marlene vibrated with dangerous potential.

"Everyone calm down," Ariana said firmly, surprised at the strength in her voice. "We can't turn on each other. Not now."

"Oh, how convenient," Reed muttered. "Exactly what the guilty person would say."

Damon stepped forward, shielding Ariana. "Watch your mouth."

Reed glared. "Your wife keeps smelling things no one else does. You keep acting like something here is about you. Maybe there's more going on."

A cold shock rippled through Ariana.

Damon stilled.

Eric turned to them. "You two walked in already on edge. You knew something about this place or about this corpse—"

"No," Ariana interrupted. "We didn't know anything. We're trying to stay alive. Just like everyone else."

But Reed's suspicion hung in the air.

Damon's breath hitched. Ariana recognized the sound.

The warning, the panic rising beneath the surface.

She grabbed his hand and squeezed hard. "It's okay. Stay with me. Don't let him pull you in."

Damon moved to her side and closed his eyes briefly before speaking to Reed. "We're not your enemies."

The older man didn't look convinced.

Tension thickened the dimness until it felt like another body in the room with them.

A faint scraping sound echoed from somewhere outside. The hallway. Something dragging along the floor..

Kaylee gulped. Lana inched closer to Ariana, her breath trembling.

"How long until we suffocate in here?" Lana whispered.

"We're not suffocating," Marlene snapped.

"We could break the window," Eric said.

"Try it," Marlene murmured, tone eerie. "They're reinforced. This was a psychiatric wing."

Ariana's stomach lurched. "You didn't mention that before."

"No one asked," Marlene said.

"So helpful." Reed growled.

Damon took a step toward Reed again, his protectiveness flaring.

Ariana caught his sleeve. "Stop, please."

He forced himself back, breathing hard.

A soft, rhythmic tapping began somewhere deeper in the building.

Like footsteps or knuckles on a sheet of metal. Perhaps someone pacing.

No one moved.

The generator coughed once.

Twice.

Then the lights flickered weakly, sputtering through the room in rapid bursts of illumination.

Flash!

Everyone shielded their eyes.

Flash.

Reed grabbed Eric's arm.

Flash.

Marlene stared at the doorway, lips parted.

Flash.

Kaylee buried her face in Ariana's leg.

Flash.

Damon pulled Ariana closer.

Flash.

And then the lights steadied. Humming and weak. But on.

Ariana blinked until the room came into focus.

"Okay," Wendy whispered, her voice shaky. "Okay, that's... better, right?"

But Ariana froze, breath locking in her throat.

Because someone was missing.

"Lana?" she called softly.

No answer.

"Lana?" Kaylee echoed, voice rising with panic.

Everyone looked around.

Where Lana had been, there was only an empty patch of floor, her backpack still lying exactly where she'd dropped it.

Damon's flashlight swung toward the hallway.

The door stood open.

And Lana was gone.

Chapter Eighteen

For a moment, the only sound in the break room was the generator humming. Ariana forced herself to breathe. Lana was just there. How could she be gone?

The spot where she had been sitting felt like a hole torn open in the center of the room. Ariana's heart punched painfully against her ribs.

It wasn't possible, yet it was really happening.

"Where... where did she go?" Kaylee asked, her voice strained.

"She didn't go anywhere," Reed snapped. "Someone took her."

"Don't say that," Wendy hissed, pulling Kaylee close.

"How?" Damon demanded. "We were all right here."

"The power was out." Reed's eyebrows furrowed.

"But we could see with the flashlight." Damon glared back at him.

"Clearly not that well."

Eric ran a hand through his hair, eyes darting from the hallway to Marlene. "Did anyone see her leave?"

Marlene's face paled. "No. I was watching the door."

Reed scoffed. "Were you?"

Marlene bristled. "Yes, and I didn't see anything."

"Of course you didn't," Reed muttered. "Because you were waiting for this."

"Reed, stop." Ariana stepped slightly in front of Damon. "Throwing accusations won't bring Lana back."

"You make it sound like she's dead." Reed rounded on her.

"Not unless you know something I don't."

Damon's grip on her tightened.

Reed waved his hands around. "Then who do you think took her? Huh? The wind? A ghost? Someone in this room knows more than they're admitting."

Ariana's pulse stumbled. Was that directed at Damon? At her? "Or maybe she went into the hallway."

"Why would she do that?" Reed's brows knit together.

"To use the bathroom. Get some air. Anything's possible at this point."

He snorted. "Right."

Wendy stepped next to Ariana. "Maybe she wanted to get away from you. Nobody could blame her for that."

Reed's nostrils flared as he stared at Wendy.

Damon stepped forward, protective tension rolling off him. "What exactly are you implying, Reed? Why would any of us know more than we're admitting?"

Reed jabbed a finger toward him. "You keep acting like someone's hunting you. Maybe *you* know more about this killer than you're saying."

Damon's jaw clenched hard. "How would I know anything? I've never heard of this hospital before, and I sure didn't have any plans to stop here for the night. All I wanted was a romantic evening with my wife."

"Then take it." Reed gestured toward the door. "There are more than enough empty rooms."

Damon's entire body tensed, and he took a step forward.

Ariana grabbed his sleeve, her pulse hammering. "Wait."

Kaylee's thin voice cut through the room. "We have to find Lana. If she was planning on leaving, she'd have told me."

"Because you're so close to a girl you just met?" Reed sneered. "Or do you two know each other from somewhere else? If that's the case, you better start talking."

"Hey." Wendy scowled at him. "Leave her alone. She's just a kid."

"I'm almost fifteen," Kaylee muttered.

"Exactly why your dad's new best friend should leave you out of this."

Everyone spoke at once, the words of the group blending together, spiraling into one another.

Damon whistled loudly. "Arguing isn't going to get us anywhere. We need to find Lana."

Wendy nodded, voice tight but firm. "Yes, we need a plan."

Eric exhaled. "We should spread out. Carefully and cover more ground than before."

"No!" Damon barked. "No one splits up."

Reed scoffed. "Someone forgot to tell that rule to Lana."

"What's your problem?" Wendy demanded.

"I don't have a problem."

"Right."

"Enough." Ariana touched Damon's hand. "We need to figure out how we split up. Just don't panic."

"Who's panicking?" Reed cocked an eyebrow.

She bit back an angry retort. It wouldn't help anything.

After more tense back-and-forth, they settled on two groups. The first group was Damon, Ariana, Kaylee, and Wendy. The second was Eric, Reed, and Marlene.

Part of Ariana wanted to be a fly on the wall to hear what the others would say when out of earshot. But mostly she was glad to not be in a group with any of them.

Given all the grumbling, no one liked the arrangement. Everyone eyed each other as if they would snakes in tall grass.

The hallway outside was colder and darker than before. It was like a narrowing tunnel of shadow with their breaths fogging, barely visible in the emergency lights.

They moved slowly, calling Lana's name. The groups split off, and before long, the other voices drifted into silence.

"Lana!" Wendy called. "If you can hear us, say something!"

Ariana held Damon's flashlight. It jittered slightly as her hand trembled from adrenaline.

Something lay ahead on the floor.

A small rectangle. Something black and white, and out of place against the gray tile.

Ariana rushed forward, Damon right behind her.

It was a newspaper clipping. Up close, it was yellowed, corners curled.

But not random.

Her blood ran cold.

The name printed on the headline was clear as day—Cal Jones.

Damon froze beside her as if someone had pressed a gun to his spine. He whispered, "No."

Wendy's spoke from behind them. "What is it?"

The clipping trembled in Ariana's hand. "It's nothing. Just a newspaper clipping."

She stepped closer. "It might not be nothing. Let me see that."

Damon stepped between them, blocking her. "We need to focus on finding Lana."

"But that could be a clue." Wendy tried looking around him to Ariana and the clipping.

Ariana slipped the paper into her pocket before anyone else caught the name.

Wendy stared between them, confused but also clearly worried. "What was it? Just tell us."

Ariana shook her head. "Just old hospital trash. Like I said, nothing."

But Damon looked sick. Sweat beaded at his temples.

"Let me see it." Wendy's voice was loud, but it shook.

Ariana felt for her, but at the same time, she couldn't risk anyone finding out there was a strong connection between Damon and the dead body, let alone that someone was leaving clues pointing to his serial killer father.

Wendy started to speak again, but Ariana pulled her aside to where Kaylee couldn't hear. "It was a clipping about a long-gone serial killer. I don't want to freak Kaylee out."

Her eyes widened. "Good thinking. Why would that be lying around? After we found a dead body?"

Ariana shrugged. "That's a really good question, but for now we should focus on finding Lana."

Wendy nodded, looking deep in thought. Then she went over to Kaylee and put an arm around her.

Damon came over to Ariana and whispered, barely audible, "That has to be a sign. Someone planted this. Someone knows."

She squeezed his arm. There was no denying facts. "Maybe they just want to scare us."

"This is the *second* clue. The murder scene and now this. Someone isn't just messing with us. They're sending a message."

Ariana felt the undeniable weight of it. Someone knew Damon's father's name and his killings well enough to replicate one.

It couldn't be a coincidence.

A distant metal door shut somewhere in the hospital.

Hopefully it was just the other group.

But it could be something much worse.

All of this could be targeted.

Would they kill Lana if Damon didn't find her in time?

Chapter Nineteen

Wendy followed closely behind Ariana as they moved back toward the break room, her fingertips brushing Kaylee's coat every few steps to reassure herself that her daughter was still there, still safe, and still breathing. Or as safe as anyone could be in this haunted nightmare of a hospital.

Ariana and Damon were whispering again.

Wendy tried not to stare, but it was impossible not to notice. They walked side-by-side, heads angled close, Damon's hand hovering at the small of Ariana's back like he was afraid she'd vanish if he didn't touch her. Ariana whispered something too quiet for Wendy to hear, and Damon nodded sharply, jaw tight, eyes darting down the hall like he expected something to leap out.

He wasn't just being protective.

It was secrecy.

They were hiding something.

Her stomach twisted.

They had done this before. Right after finding the body.

The couple had melted into their own private corner, whispering intensely while the rest of the group reeled in shock.

At the time, Wendy assumed Damon was comforting her. Now she wasn't so sure.

They reached the break room just as Reed, Eric, and Marlene emerged from another hallway, looking tense, pale, and jumpy. Reed muttered something to Eric that sounded like *this place is a maze*, while Marlene clutched a manila folder like it might float away if she let go.

Wendy's gaze flicked to the folder. "What's that?"

Marlene hesitated. "Something we found in the old records room."

Reed crossed his arms. "Tell them."

Marlene took a shaky breath. "It's… a patient file." She held it out with trembling hands. "It was splayed open, like someone was just reading it."

Wendy's pulse spiked. "Why's that a big deal?"

"It's for a man named Cal Jones." Marlene held the file closer. "Name ring a bell?"

Kaylee shook her head. "Never heard of him."

The name hit Wendy like a slap. He was a notorious serial killer who'd supposedly offed himself in prison, though there was a lot of doubt about it actually being self-inflicted.

Or if it was a cover-up and he was actually still alive.

But that wasn't the most jarring part.

The newspaper clipping that Ariana found was about a serial killer.

Wendy turned to her, throwing her a questioning look.

Ari gave the slightest nod. And a pleading look.

She didn't want Wendy to say anything.

But it was confirmation. The clipping was about the same killer as the file the others found.

Somebody wanted them to find those items.

Reed's voice brought Wendy back to the room. "He was a serial killer. Real piece of work. Got what he had coming in prison." He turned his head and used his hand to mock a hanging.

Wendy covered Kaylee's eyes. "Stop!"

"Mom!" Kaylee squirmed away. "I know people get killed in jail, okay? I'm not a baby."

Wendy's face warmed. "You can't blame me for being protective with everything going on here. There was a killing and now this?"

Marlene hugged her elbows. "Cal was treated here. Before he was convicted."

Wendy frowned. "Why would a murderer be in a hospital like this?"

"For psychiatric evaluation," Marlene said quietly. "He was violent. Dangerous."

Reed chimed in. "Locked up after that. Died in prison, I think."

Ariana and Damon exchanged a glance.

They knew something. But what?

Wendy felt Kaylee press closer to her side.

But Wendy wasn't watching the others anymore. The moment the name Cal Jones left Marlene's lips, they both froze. It wasn't fear of the story. No, it was most definitely recognition.

Wendy wasn't imagining it.

Her spine prickled. Now the patterns screamed at her too loud to ignore.

Ariana and Damon whispered after finding the body. They whispered again after finding the clipping. And now, hearing the name of a serial killer connected to this hospital... they shared a look. A fast, loaded, and secret look.

Wendy understood something with cold clarity—the couple knew more than they were saying.

Maybe not everything. Perhaps not the whole truth.

But something they didn't want the others to know.

Wendy tightened her arm around Kaylee, gaze narrowing on the two people standing too still, too quietly at the edge of the room.

She decided, right then and there, that she was going to find out exactly what they were hiding.

Because in this place—with a missing girl, a fresh corpse, and a killer's file appearing out of thin air—secrets could get them all killed.

The last thing she was going to do was allow anything to happen to her or her daughter.

Chapter Twenty

Ariana glanced over at Wendy. Still staring at her and Damon. The woman had obviously made a connection between the newspaper clipping and the file, but there was no way she could figure out Damon's relation to Cal.

They hadn't shared their last name with anyone. It was something they were careful about in general, even though Jones was a common surname.

Reed and Eric flipped through the patient file. Marlene hovered near the doorway with that unsettling stillness she carried like armor. Kaylee sat trembling next to her mother. Ariana felt the weight of Wendy's gaze lingering on her and Damon.

She knew they were hiding something. But she couldn't possibly know what.

Ariana kept her expression neutral, but her pulse spiked.

Wendy wasn't just scared anymore. She was studying them.

Damon shifted beside her, fingers tapping anxiously

against the flashlight. His movements weren't measured. Not the controlled worry he usually carried. Tonight it was sharper, rawer. His shoulders tensed with every passing second.

"You okay?" she whispered.

He nodded stiffly, but she didn't believe him. Not with the clipping in her pocket, and not with the patient file that made Damon go quiet and rigid, shadows collecting around his eyes.

Not with the storm pounding the windows like angry fists.

Reed shut the file. "This is insane. We're wandering around an abandoned psych ward with a killer reenacting old crimes, and one of us is missing. We need to do something."

Damon tensed.

They exchanged a glance. Reed knew about the death being a copycat of Cal's.

Was it only a matter of time before the others figured out their connection to the infamous murderer?

Eric rubbed the bridge of his nose. "Do what, Reed? There's no cell reception. The roads are buried. Doors are locking themselves."

"Not themselves," Reed snapped. "Someone's locking them."

Everyone stared at Marlene.

She stiffened. "I didn't do anything"

Reed's voice grew louder. "Why should we believe you? You know the hall layouts. You know about the reinforced windows. You knew this killer Jones was connected to the hospital."

Marlene's voice sharpened. "Because I worked here. Of course I knew—everyone did. Don't ask me why we found his file now. It isn't like he's the only well-known patient that was treated here. You act like I planned this, but I was as shocked as everyone else."

Damon stepped toward Reed, his hands in tight fists. "Enough. You're wasting time blaming the wrong people."

Reed folded his arms. "How do *you* know who the wrong people are?"

Damon's jaw ticked, his breathing harsher than before, his shoulders rigid. He wasn't just mad. He was afraid that someone was getting too close to the wrong truth.

She touched his sleeve. "Damon, leave it alone."

"No." His voice cracked at the edges. "I'm not letting him corner her."

Reed squared up. "Corner who, Damon? Marlene? Or Ariana?"

Ariana drew in a deep breath. "Reed, stop. We need to work together if we're going to find Lana. She's still missing, remember? We're focused on a dead serial killer, and one of our group has mysteriously vanished."

"Oh, I'm sorry," Reed said with a humorless laugh. "Are we not allowed to notice the two of you whispering every time something creepy happens?"

Damon stepped closer, tension radiating off him like heat from a furnace. "Are you accusing us of something?"

Wendy pulled Kaylee behind her, eyes wide.

Eric reached for Reed's arm. "Stop antagonizing him."

Reed ignored him. "What's your deal, Damon? You know something? You hiding something? It's starting to seem that way."

Damon's hands curled into fists again.

Ariana grabbed one quickly. "Breathe. Stay with me. Don't let him get to you."

He tried. She saw him try. But the storm outside roared louder, punching against the walls in violent gusts that made the building shudder.

A low rumbling traveled through the floor. Snow sliding off the roof? Or something heavier collapsing outside?

Wendy shivered, pulling Kaylee closer. "The storm's getting worse. We should shelter in a room without windows that could break."

Marlene scowled. "They're reinforced. I told you."

Eric peered through the narrow gap in the blinds. "Visibility's nothing. I can't see the parking lot anymore."

Ariana followed his gaze. The windows rattled as wind whipped snow in tight circles—swirling, fast, almost unnatural. Flashes of white streaked across the glass.

"We can't stay here." Reed said it as if Wendy hadn't just said the same thing. "We need to find Lana before the lights go out again."

A sharp crack split the air.

Everyone froze.

Then a second crack. Louder, deep, and splintering.

Marlene paled. "That's the glass."

Reed scoffed. "You said the windows are reinforced."

"I didn't say they were impenetrable."

As if on cue, the window nearest the hallway exploded inward, shards of glass shattering like brittle ice. A large branch stuck half inside and half outside.

Kaylee screamed. Eric yanked her back.

Ariana flinched as wind blasted through the break room, spraying snow and debris in a violent rush.

Something landed on the floor with a sickening thud at the center of the room.

Damon's flashlight rolled across the ground, spinning wildly, the beam slicing through chaos and stopping on a single object lying among the shattered glass.

A white hospital wristband attached to a brick.

Covered in snow.

Hide and Seek

And printed with one name. Lana White.

Ariana's breath left her body.

The storm wasn't the worst thing outside.

Someone had just thrown a wristband with Lana's name through a reinforced window.

Had she been a patient here too? Was White even her last name?

There was only one way to find out.

Chapter Twenty-One

Snow gusted through the broken window, slicing the air with icy needles. Though the tension in the room was much colder. Ariana shivered more from that than the broken window.

Kaylee cried softly into Wendy's coat, and Eric stayed near them, patting Kaylee's back. His face flattened into a grim mask as he looked around the room.

Ariana crouched to pick up Lana's backpack, her fingers trembling as she zipped it closed. Damon grabbed her coat, his duffel, and the half-charged flashlight, moving with quick, jerky motions that betrayed the crack in his composure. Every time the wind howled through the shattered glass, he flinched.

Wendy stuffed the patient file into her coat protectively, as if she thought someone else might take it and hide it.

Reed kicked aside a shard of thick glass. "This is getting worse. We can't stay in a room with a blown-out window."

Marlene spun on him. "And going deeper into the hospital is somehow safer?"

Hide and Seek

"At least the halls still have doors," Reed shot back. "And walls! And not that." He gestured to the broken window.

"It wasn't the storm," Marlene snapped. "Someone threw that wristband, and the windows *are* reinforced."

"So you admit someone's here," Reed snarled. "Someone maybe you know?"

Marlene stepped closer, face contorting. "I don't know anything. You think I'd be here if I thought someone dangerous was wandering the halls?"

"That's a lie." Reed stared her down. "Everything about you is suspicious. Your keys, your calm, the way you stare down hallways like you're waiting for someone to pop out. For all any of us knows, you and Lana are working together."

"That's ridiculous! I'm a nurse, Reed. I *save* lives. Not threaten them. And Lana is just a girl. What harm could she do?"

"Plenty if she really wanted to. You could be—"

"Enough." Ariana glared at him. "We don't have time for this."

Damon joined her, breathing fast but steady enough to speak. "We still need to find Lana. She's out there, and whoever broke that window took her. This isn't finished."

Wendy clung to Kaylee's shoulders, shivering. "We have to move. This room is freezing."

Eric nodded. "Let's go. We search the rest of the wing then find a secure place to regroup."

Reed scoffed. "And if Lana's in danger right now?"

Eric's jaw tightened. "We don't split up again."

The wind answered for them with another blast that sent papers flying from the counter.

Ariana grabbed Damon's sleeve. "You ready?"

His eyes were distant, pupils blown wide, breath shallow. He was spiraling.

Even after all these years, just mentioning his father brought back so much trauma. Cal Jones had ruined so many lives, including his own son's.

But Damon took Ariana's hand and squeezed. "I'm not letting you out of my sight."

Wendy glanced at them with another of her quiet, measured looks—but said nothing.

Ariana and Damon were the first to step into the hall. Not surprisingly, the corridor was warmer than the break room—not that it was warm.

Their footsteps echoed as they walked, bouncing down the empty hall.

Emergency lights flickered overhead, long sputtering beams that made shadows strobe and dance.

Kaylee pointed a trembling finger at a peeling sign on the wall.

WING C – Restricted Access
BASEMENT LEVEL (Old Ward)

Eric frowned. "There's a basement?"

Ariana shuddered at the thought.

Marlene stiffened. "It was closed off decades ago."

Reed snorted. "Which means that's exactly where creeps hide."

Wendy muttered, "It would take one to know one."

He didn't appear to have heard her. That was a small blessing. The last thing the group needed was more arguing.

"Mental patients stayed down there," Marlene said. "There are seclusion rooms, old surgical areas, and even a now-defunct morgue."

Kaylee whimpered.

Wendy wrapped her arms around the girl and shot a look of annoyance at the older woman. "Can we not talk about morgues?"

"I'm just stating facts."

Damon inhaled sharply. "This place gets worse by the minute."

Ariana squeezed his hand. "Focus on your breathing."

He tried.

Reed turned to him. "You've been jumpy since that body. I didn't take you for the type."

"Leave him alone," Ariana snapped. "Let's just focus on finding Lana. *Everyone* is on edge right now."

He grumbled something under his breath but at least dropped it.

They walked past the area where the men found the body. Damon avoided the doorway completely, jaw clenching as the memories flickered across his face.

Ariana stayed close, touching him as an anchor.

Marlene slowed near a set of double doors that looked newer than the rest of the building. The paint was fresher than the rest.

Eric frowned. "These were replaced recently."

Reed pushed the door slightly. It didn't move. "It's locked. From the inside."

Ariana's breath hitched. "Someone could be hiding in there. Or holding Lana there."

Damon shook his head. "There's no light coming from underneath."

"Maybe it leads somewhere else." Reed squared his jaw.

Marlene's voice dropped to a whisper. "It leads to the stairwell for the basement."

"Bingo," Reed said. "We're going."

"What?" Wendy pulled her daughter even closer. "Kaylee and I are most certainly not going down there."

"No," Marlene insisted, panic threading her tone. "The stairs are unstable. They're old, rusted, and dangerous."

Reed smirked. "Funny, everything dangerous in this hospital is something you 'just happen' to know about."

Marlene stepped back, shaking her head. "I worked here for a long time. You should be more worried if I *didn't* know anything about this place."

A sound rang out from behind the locked double doors.

Ariana froze.

Not a falling tray, not wind.

A footstep.

Damon grabbed her arm and held her tight, flashlight aimed at the door. "Someone's in there."

Kaylee sniffled again. Wendy wrapped both arms around her, eyes wide and glassy. "We need to go somewhere else."

Reed shoved his shoulder into the door. Not once but twice, however the metal didn't budge.

Eric pulled him away. "If someone's in there, they don't want us coming in."

"Or they want us separated," Damon said, voice shaking. "Look at the angles. There's no clear line of sight. Someone could—"

A loud thud shook the door from the inside as if someone slammed their whole body against it.

Reed yelped and jumped back.

"Now who's jumpy?" Damon asked.

"We're not opening that," Wendy whispered.

"No," Damon agreed. "Not until we know what's on the other side."

The odd odor from before tickled Ariana's nose. It was faint but unmistakable.

Damon turned to her. "Ari?"

"It's back," she whispered.

Reed shivered. "What the hell does that mean?"

Before anyone could answer, a door at the far end of the hall clicked. Then creaked.

It opened slowly into darkness.

Ariana stiffened.

Marlene paled. "None of the doors can open on their own."

Ariana stepped closer to Damon, heart pounding in her throat.

Eric pressed himself against the wall. "What if another window broke?"

Marlene frowned. "Still unlikely."

That meant someone wasn't just inside the building. They were close. And they might not be working alone.

Chapter Twenty-Two

The door at the end of the hall groaned wider, the shadows behind it pulsing with cold air. Ariana clung to Damon's arm as the others froze.

Reed stepped toward the noise. "We need to check that out."

But then a choked sound came from behind the locked double doors.

A person. It sounded feminine.

Then came a scream, high pitched and unmistakably human.

Kaylee cried out. Wendy grabbed her, pressing her close.

Reed spun toward Marlene. "Your keys. Now!"

Marlene backed away, clutching them to her chest. "That door isn't safe."

Reed lunged, ripping the keyring from her trembling hands.

Marlene stared as if frozen in place.

He shoved them back at her, shaking, his eyes filled with panic.

She forced herself forward, trying each key with trembling fingers.

Another yelp sounded behind the door. Banging. Clangs.

A struggle.

Something heavy hit the other side of the wall.

Ariana's heart shot into her throat. "She's in trouble. Hurry!"

Damon pressed his palm against the door as if he could reach her through it. "Hang on! We're coming."

"Mom," Kaylee whimpered into Wendy's side. "Don't go. Please don't go in there."

Wendy's eyes went wide with raw, maternal terror. "I… I can't take you in there."

Reed turned sharply. "Then you'll be on your own when whoever's behind this comes back."

She looked like she'd been slapped. Then she looked around, her gaze landing on her daughter. "Kaylee, I'm sorry. I can't leave you out here either. We all need to stay as a group."

Kaylee leaned close, and Wendy tried to shield her eyes.

Marlene's key clicked.

The lock turned.

A hot wave of dread washed over Ariana.

Reed shoved open the door.

Cold, damp air rushed out. A concrete stairwell plunged downward into pale-yellow emergency lighting. The smell hit Ariana immediately. She gagged, clutching Damon's arm.

Damon swallowed hard, his face ashen. "Ari, stay behind me."

From below sounded scraping, followed by a gasp.

Then silence.

"Lana!" Damon yelled, echoing down the stairwell.

No answer.

Reed charged forward. "She's down there."

"Reed, wait," Ariana cried, but he was already bounding down the stairs, flashlight swinging wildly.

Damon dragged her with him, one arm around her waist, keeping her anchored.

The stairwell opened into a long, low-ceilinged corridor. Old peeling signs pointed to Seclusion Rooms, Storage, and Patient Holding.

Reed's flashlight jerked ahead of them. "Over here!"

A breath caught in Ariana's throat as they rushed forward.

Lana lay crumpled against a wall, one hand stretched outward, her hair covering her face. Her chest didn't rise. Her stillness was absolute. Final.

Ariana froze.

Wendy gasped and shielded Kaylee's eyes.

Eric stumbled back.

Marlene turned away with a strangled sound.

Not again, not another death. Not Lana, who had clung to her only hours ago.

Damon reached Lana first, kneeling beside her. He touched her neck gently. "No pulse." His shoulders sagged, shaking. "She's gone."

Ariana pressed a hand to her mouth, tears burning behind her eyes.

Reed punched the wall, forehead pressed to it. "She was alive just minutes ago!"

Kaylee sobbed into Wendy's coat.

Eric bent down slowly, jaw trembling. "Look at her hand."

Ariana's breath stopped.

Damon reached out and carefully unclasped Lana's fingers.

A tightly folded, damp square of old newsprint slipped free.

Eric held the flashlight steady as Marlene unfolded it with shaking hands.

It was another newspaper clipping. This one was yellowed and fragile, older than the first one. The one only Ariana and Damon had seen.

The headline was about Cal Jones again. But this one mentioned his son. Damon's name wasn't listed, but it mentioned him directly.

A chill sliced through Ariana's ribs.

Damon swayed as he read it, face draining of color.

Ariana grabbed him, holding him up.

Reed blinked at Damon. "What's wrong now?"

Wendy narrowed her eyes. "Why are you two reacting like that?"

Ariana's heart hammered. "One of our own is dead! How do you expect us to react? Especially with this being the second body tonight."

Even with all of that being true, Wendy saw them. She knew about the first clipping.

Would she say something to the others?

Damon exchanged a worried glance with Ariana. Someone had brought them here, staged reenactments, and left clues.

Left bodies.

And now used Lana to send another message. A direct one.

Ariana shuddered.

Somebody in this building knew Damon was Cal's son.

The basement lights flickered overhead.

Somewhere deeper in the dark, a door closed.

Ariana clutched Damon's hand, pulse roaring in her ears.

This wasn't random, wasn't the storm. Wasn't a coincidence.

They were being hunted.

Chapter Twenty-Three

Wendy couldn't get the image of Lana's dead body out of her head. She had shielded Kaylee's eyes, but she'd seen it too. The group had moved away from the corpse, but the fact that one of them had died hung in the air like ice.

That wasn't all. That quick, sharp flicker of shock between Ariana and Damon when they read the clipping. Not horror or grief, but recognition.

It stayed with her as they gathered in the dim, low-ceilinged corridor of the basement, everyone trembling from cold, fear, or both.

Kaylee clung to Wendy with one hand while Wendy stroked her daughter's hair like when she was little, but her focus kept drifting back to the couple whispering again. Those two were always whispering, always stepping away from the others.

What did they know? Why did the name in that clipping hit them so hard?

Hide and Seek

Wendy needed answers. She needed to protect herself and Kaylee. She shifted her weight, pulling her daughter just slightly behind her as she watched Ariana and Damon speak in hushed, frantic tones.

Damon's head bowed close to Ariana's, shoulders clenched, fists trembling. Ariana kept touching his arm, his back, steadying him. They looked terrified, but not just of Lana's death.

Of the meaning behind it.

Wendy studied them and tried to hear their whispers.

But that was impossible because Reed was loudly pacing like a caged animal, raking both hands through his hair. Eric stood at a distance, staring at nothing with a haunted hollowness. He wouldn't even check on his family because he was so wrapped up in himself.

Typical.

And Marlene seemed to be unraveling. She had slumped against the wall, keys dangling loosely from her hand. Her breathing came in short, gasping pulls. Her tight composure cracked right down the middle. "Cal Jones. I knew him."

Silence shadowed the corridor.

Reed spun toward her, eyes blazing. "What did you just say?"

Marlene flinched like she'd been slapped. "Not him. I mean... I met his family. When he was brought here for evaluation."

Eric stepped closer, his brows furrowing. "You met the killer's family? And you didn't think to mention this before, when we found the file?"

Marlene nodded jerkily. "They came to sign papers. His wife and their boy. A little boy... jumpy, quiet. He wouldn't look at anyone. Always hiding behind his mother."

Wendy's pulse pounded. "What was his name?"

Marlene shook her head. "I don't remember. It was so long ago. Jones is a common name. And we weren't supposed to discuss patients with anyone, especially the criminal ones." She covered her face with shaking hands. "I only remember his eyes. Big and dark. Scared."

Reed took a threatening step toward her. "So you have a connection to Cal Jones, and you just happen to show up in the storm? You knew all this and didn't warn anyone?"

Marlene's voice cracked. "I didn't know any of this was happening again. I didn't."

"This is targeted at you. You're bringing all of this chaos and death to the rest of us."

"No!" Marlene shook her head violently. "He wouldn't have targeted me. I didn't matter since I was just a nurse's aide then. I filed charts, mopped floors, brought food. That's it. He probably never even noticed me."

"You're hiding something," Reed accused. "You must be."

Everyone's attention swung to Marlene.

Wendy's didn't. She watched Ariana and Damon.

Ariana hugged Damon's arm to her, whispering at him to breathe, to stay grounded. Damon kept shaking his head as though he couldn't shirk off the past.

Wendy's skin prickled.

Because if Marlene really didn't remember the boy's name, why did Damon and Ariana look like they knew it?

A cold realization crept into Wendy's chest, sharp and undeniable. Ariana and Damon weren't just scared. They were implicated somehow.

Their secret wasn't small.

And whatever they weren't telling the group, it had to be dangerous.

Wendy hugged Kaylee closer, her heartbeat a frantic drum.

Whatever was happening in this hospital and whoever set all this in motion, Ariana and Damon were at the center of it.

And Wendy wasn't going to stop until she found out why.

Chapter Twenty-Four

Ariana couldn't take her attention from Wendy. She knew about the first clipping and had stayed quiet about that even after the file about Cal Jones had been discovered.

But now she looked like she was going to burst. Wendy wasn't subtle, and now her stare was sharper. It wasn't just fear anymore. It was scrutiny. Calculating. Like she was trying to piece together a puzzle she didn't even know she had all the pieces for.

Damon leaned against the wall behind Ariana, rubbing his palms against his jeans, breath too shallow. She brushed his arm gently, grounding him as best she could. But she felt how tightly wound he was. Each sound made him flinch, every shadow made him coil like something inside him was trying to break free.

Wendy watched that too.

Ariana exhaled and stepped toward her. "Can we talk? Just for a second?"

Wendy hesitated before nodding, guiding Kaylee just a bit

behind her but staying within sight of the others.

Ariana led her a few feet away, far enough for space but still close enough for safety.

Wendy folded her arms. "You two keep whispering to each other. You're reacting like you know more than the rest of us."

Ariana forced her shoulders to relax. She needed to distract Wendy from whatever she was thinking. It was clear she was getting too close to the truth. "We're just scared. Everyone is."

"That's not all it is." Wendy's jaw tensed. "You went pale at that name of Cal. And Damon... he's falling apart. More than the situation calls for."

"We have two dead bodies. No reaction is out of line."

Wendy took a deep breath. "You two didn't tell the others about the first news clipping. Why?"

Ariana froze. Damon's tremors, the way he'd nearly lunged at Reed twice now, the haunted look when Marlene mentioned the little boy in the hospital hall all those years ago... she couldn't deny any of it.

But she couldn't tell Wendy the truth—not here. Not now. Not with Lana dead two rooms away and the killer somewhere nearby listening to every word.

Ariana stepped closer. "Wendy, look. I don't know why this hospital has ties to Cal Jones. I don't know why someone here seems to be... reenacting things connected to him." Not entirely a lie, not entirely the truth. "But I do know Marlene just gave us something real. She met his family. That means she knows more than she's letting on."

Wendy's expression flickered with fear mixing with a sudden, sharp understanding. "You think she's involved."

"I think," Ariana said carefully, "that someone is using this place's history. And Marlene's history is the only clear link we have right now."

Wendy glanced past Ariana, eyes drawn involuntarily back

to Damon. "And the two of you? What's *your* link? You can't deny there's something. We can't risk anyone else dying, so you have to say what you know. At least to me. I've already proven I'll keep your secrets, and I need to keep my daughter safe. Surely, you can understand that."

She had a point. But that didn't mean she could tell her about Damon being Cal's son. That wasn't her story to spill. Ariana's pulse stumbled. She opened her mouth. She needed to say something, some half-truth that would soothe Wendy without exposing Damon.

A sound erupted from deep in the basement. Some low metallic scrape. Long, dragging.

Like something heavy pulled across concrete.

Wendy's breath hitched. "What was *that?*"

Ariana turned sharply, grabbing her arm. "Stay close."

Reed spun around, flashlight jerking wildly. "It's coming from down the corridor."

Marlene whispered something under her breath and backed up to the wall, hands pressed flat against the peeling paint.

Eric tightened his grip on the flashlight, eyes wide. "Someone's down there."

Damon straightened behind Ariana, his trembling stilled in an instant. "Who's that?"

Kaylee whimpered and pressed herself against Wendy, who wrapped both arms around her.

The dragging sound came again.

Closer.

A slow, steady scrape echoing through the long, barely lit basement corridor. Like someone pulling a chair. Or a body bag. Or...

Ariana didn't let herself finish the thought. She grabbed Damon's hand.

Reed whispered, voice cracking, "Whatever that is... it's coming *toward* us."

The emergency lights flickered once.

Again.

The scraping stopped.

Silence spliced through the basement, heavy and suffocating.

Ariana's heart thudded in her throat.

From the darkness ahead came a single, deliberate knock on metal.

Chapter Twenty-Five

The pounding sound still vibrated in Ariana's bones when Reed spoke up. "We need to check that out."

Eric stiffened. "If someone's down here, they could be holding something… or someone."

Reed nodded. "We have numbers on our side."

Damon's grip on Ariana's hand tightened. He looked at her the way he always did right before doing something reckless and self-sacrificing. "I'm going."

"No." Ariana's chest seized. "Stay with me."

Reed cut her off. "We'll go. The three of us. You women take Kaylee and get upstairs where it's safe."

Kaylee jolted at the word "women," her fingers bunching in Wendy's sleeve. "Mom, don't let them go alone."

Wendy held her tightly, but her eyes darted to the dark corridor with open fear. "We're not leaving them, honey. We're giving them space to investigate. We're just relocating. To a safer place."

Ariana recognized the lie, spoken with a mother's desperation.

Marlene cleared her throat. "There's a kitchen on the main floor. It has a pantry. It was stocked with non-perishables—canned goods, sealed snacks. If no one's scavenged it since closure, we might find something."

Reed snorted. "Perfect. Let the ladies go grab some granola bars while we check out the murder wing."

Ariana shot him a withering glare.

Damon stepped between them, shoulders tense. "Watch your tone, Reed."

He rolled his eyes but backed off. "Whatever. Let's go."

Eric steadied his flashlight.

Damon cupped Ariana's cheek with trembling fingers, his breath warm and uneven. "Stay with them. Don't go anywhere alone. Not for a second. Promise?"

His voice cracked on the last word.

Ariana nodded, pressing her hand over his. "And you stay with the guys. No heroics. Promise?"

Damon gave a hollow laugh. "Too late for that."

She kissed the back of his hand, quickly, desperately. "Come back to me safe and sound."

He squeezed her fingers hard, then tore himself away with the others. Reed charged ahead, Eric close behind, and Damon trailing just long enough to look back at her as though memorizing her face.

Then the men disappeared down the corridor, engulfed by darkness and echoing silence.

Ariana's pulse thrummed loud in her ears.

Wendy straightened, smoothing Kaylee's hair with shaking hands. "Come on. Let's go before they hear something else. And don't look at the body. I'm serious."

Kaylee nodded.

As they headed up the stairs, the girl kept her head turned away from her friend's body. They ascended the basement stairs quickly, Kaylee clutching the railing like each step might vanish beneath her.

When they reached the main level, Marlene pointed down the hall, her eyes wide and glassy. "Kitchen's this way. Past the old exam rooms."

Ariana instinctively placed herself between Wendy and Marlene. Close enough to shield, far enough to keep an eye on the woman whose connection to Cal Jones seemed to grow murkier by the minute.

The lights flickered. A soft, rhythmic tapping echoed somewhere above them.

Wendy stiffened. "Tell me that's the storm."

Marlene didn't answer.

They started down the hall toward the kitchen, their footsteps sounding too loud against the sterile tile.

The building groaned, settling in ways that felt unnatural. A door creaked shut on its own. A distant clang reverberated through the ducts.

Kaylee whimpered. "Why does everything sound alive?"

Ariana patted her back gently. "It's an old building. Metal expands and contracts in storms."

But even as she said it, she didn't believe herself.

The storm outside howled through unseen cracks. The emergency lights flickered overhead. Generators hummed and sputtered. Somewhere behind them, Ariana swore she heard whispering. Soft, frantic, overlapping voices like someone speaking through a wall.

It had to be her imagination.

Wendy grabbed her arm. "Did you hear that?"

Ari's breath hitched. "Yes."

Marlene's pace quickened, keys jangling at her hip. "Kitchen's just ahead. We're almost there."

A sharp bang echoed from the hallway they'd just left.

Kaylee shrieked, jumping into her mother's arms.

Wendy's voice cracked. "Hurry."

They hurried around the corner, past the old nurses' station and toward a swinging metal door labeled KITCHEN – STAFF ONLY.

Marlene shouldered it open.

Ariana glanced back down the hall. Empty.

But that didn't soothe her. Every instinct in her body whispered that they weren't being followed.

They were being hunted.

Chapter Twenty Six

Damon stayed several paces behind Reed, every muscle in his body tight enough to snap. His flashlight beam trembled over peeling paint and rusted hinges as they moved deeper into the basement corridor.

Eric whispered, "I hate this. I hate this so much."

Reed kept barreling forward like he had something to prove. "Keep it together. If something's down here, I want eyes on it before it comes after the women."

Damon's jaw clenched. "Don't talk about them like they're helpless."

Reed threw him a look over his shoulder. "I'm talking about the kid, Damon."

Damon didn't answer.

Couldn't.

The corridor around them felt too narrow, too suffocating. The air colder than it should've been. His pulse hammered in his throat, chest tight with a familiar pressure—the old panic, the one that clawed up from his childhood when he thought about his father, about the nightmares that still broke him open in the dark from living with a monster who'd stolen his mother from him.

Every shadow seemed to contain his father's silhouette.

Each draft carried Cal's shadow.

But he kept going. For Ariana. For the baby. For the chance that they could save everyone else in their group. Even though they'd been unable to help Lana.

He blinked hard, pushing the memory of her stillness out of his mind.

Reed stopped abruptly, holding up a hand. "Hear that?"

Damon froze, breath lodged high in his chest.

At the end of the hall, a faint scrape, like something being dragged.

Again.

Damon swallowed hard, trying to ground himself. "It's the same sound we heard before."

Reed nodded. "Means whatever moved down here might still be close."

Eric gripped his flashlight tighter. "Or it's hiding."

"Yeah," Reed muttered. "That too."

They moved slowly, cautiously, until they reached the corridor's dead end—two storage doors chained shut and an old records room with a flickering light inside.

The scraping sound stopped as they approached.

Reed raised his flashlight, stepping toward the open doorway of the records room.

Damon felt a chill roll down his back. "Don't. This is exactly how people die in movies."

Reed ignored him and pushed the door fully open.

Eric muttered something under his breath.

The room was empty.

Not just empty, but cleared out. Every cabinet yanked

open. Files dumped across the floor in haphazard piles. Drawers overturned. Paper everywhere like snowfall.

Eric cleared his throat. "Someone was searching for something."

Damon's pulse roared. "Or leaving with something."

Reed walked slowly to a pile of papers, nudging them aside with his boot. "Look at this."

Damon approached, dread tightening his chest, every heartbeat a warning he didn't know how to heed.

Reed crouched and lifted a thin manila folder from the floor. It was pristine compared to the others scattered around it. Placed deliberately.

The label, scrawled in faded ink:

PATIENT FILE: JONES, CAL – CHILD EVALUATION MATERIALS

Damon's vision tunneled.

Eric frowned. "Child evaluation?"

Reed opened it.

Inside were only two things. A page torn from a psychological assessment, describing Cal's potential for "multigenerational transmission of violent pathology" and a photocopied photo. It was grainy and old.

A woman whose arms were around a boy with big, dark eyes.

Damon's knees nearly buckled.

The caption under the photo read:

Jones Family Son.

Reed blinked. "Why would they have this down here?"

Eric shook his head. "For us to find?"

Damon couldn't breathe.

It felt like his father's fingers were closing around his throat.

Reed looked up at him, eyes narrowing. "Why does this freak you out so much?"

Damon forced his voice steady. "Because someone is taunting us. Leaving clues and playing with us."

Reed scoffed. "And you seem to be taking it personally."

Damon's control slipped just a fraction. "A girl died. Two people, actually—"

Eric's voice cut in. "Look at the picture again."

Damon's stomach turned.

Eric pointed to something underneath the boy in the photo. "Damon?"

His name was written in faded ink underneath the little boy in the picture.

Damon couldn't answer. He couldn't lie.

Those were his eyes, his hair. His mother's sweater.

His entire childhood in a snapshot he never knew existed.

A secret the world wasn't supposed to know.

Reed's expression shifted with unease threading through suspicion. "Was that you? Damon isn't exactly a popular name."

Damon backed away from the photo as if it would burn him. "Someone is using Cal's history. Someone who knows—" *Who I am*, he almost said. *Who my father was.*

Eric stepped forward. "What's your last name? Is it Jones?"

Damon's breath shook uncontrollably.

Reed huffed. "Don't bother answering. We need to get back to the others. Now."

But Damon couldn't move.

Because now he couldn't deny the truth any longer.

Someone had planned this.

Curated it.

Built a trap for him to step into.

Every corridor, every clue, every body.

Targeted.

At him.

And whoever did it was escalating.

Chapter Twenty Seven

Wendy's breath hitched as they entered the kitchen. It was darker than she'd expected with high industrial ceilings, rows of stainless-steel counters, pots still hanging like forgotten skeletons. The storm moaned against the walls, vibrating metal racks. Kaylee stayed stuck to her side, fingers curled tight in Wendy's sleeve.

She had to admit she liked her daughter turning to her now, even if there were less options now with Lana gone. Her chest tightened at the thought. The young woman had been killed—right before they could get to her.

Now there were less of them in the group. They had to stick closer than before.

Marlene pushed open a swinging door, revealing a walk-in pantry. It smelled like old plastic, but shelves lined the walls with cans, sealed bags, and industrial-sized containers that looked untouched since the place closed.

"We might have enough for a night or two," Marlene murmured, holding her flashlight high.

Ariana exhaled. "Thank God."

Hopefully they wouldn't need more than that. Wendy didn't want to think about staying here longer than a night. She scanned the pantry, but her attention was already shifting because Marlene was acting off again. The woman hadn't been too quick to answer, and she kept looking away when Wendy's gaze landed on her.

Kaylee grabbed two granola bars and shoved them into her pocket.

Wendy gently smoothed her hair. "We'll get you something warm later, okay?"

She nodded, pulling closer.

Wendy turned to Marlene. "Start talking."

Marlene blinked. "About what?"

"You know what." Wendy stepped toward her, forcing Marlene back a half-step. "Cal Jones. His family. All of it."

Ariana stiffened noticeably.

Interesting.

"You said you met them," Wendy pressed. "You saw them here. Fine. But how much did you really know? Did they tell you anything? Did you overhear an important conversation? See anything of interest?"

"It was close to twenty years ago. How much do you remember from that long ago?"

"Plenty." Wendy wasn't about to let her change the subject.

Marlene cleared her throat. "I was an aide. I brought water, filed notes. I wasn't supposed to talk to them."

"But you did. You said you remembered the boy's eyes."

"I remember trauma. It sticks in the mind more than anything.."

Wendy narrowed her eyes. "And what *else* sticks in yours?"

Marlene faltered. "I... I don't know."

"You do," Wendy insisted. "You're not telling us everything."

Ariana reached out cautiously. "Stop. She's scared."

"So am I." Wendy's voice cracked. "So is Kaylee. And worse, Lana's dead. Somebody is hunting us and using a serial killer's history to do so. We're not going to survive this if everyone keeps holding secrets."

Ariana froze. "We need to eat."

Wendy turned her attention directly to Ariana. "You keep whispering with Damon. Every time something awful happens, you two slip into your own little world and panic together. Why?"

"Because we're married. We have a long history together."

"How long could it be? You're, what, twenty-six at most?"

"We've been together over ten years. Why does that matter?"

Wendy remembered being that young. It wasn't that long ago, though the years since motherhood had flown by in a blink. Now that she was in her forties, problems from her twenties seemed so miniscule.

Kaylee looked between them with wide, frightened eyes.

Wendy pressed on. "What are you hiding?"

Ariana stepped closer, lowering her voice. "Wendy, this isn't the time."

"It is exactly the time." Wendy's hands shook, but she didn't stop. "I'm trying to protect my daughter, and I can't do that if you and Damon are keeping something from the rest of us."

Ariana hesitated a beat too long.

Wendy felt something snake down her spine. "Why did you hesitate?"

Ariana opened her mouth.

The lights above them flickered again.

Not an outage, not the generator failing.

A pulse. One, two, three.

Then the metallic sound from earlier echoed down the kitchen hall.

Dragging. A slow, heavy scrape.

Kaylee gasped, gripping Wendy's arm hard enough to bruise. "Mom!"

Ariana went rigid, wrapping her arms around herself. "We have to stay together. Our group is already cut in half."

Marlene backed toward the pantry door, knees buckling. "He's coming up here."

"He, who?" Ariana asked.

"Whoever's after us," Marlene quipped.

Wendy's heart thundered in her ears. She whispered the question again, raw and trembling. "Ariana, what aren't you telling us?"

But with the scraping sound getting nearer, that might not be the most important question.

They needed to stay safe. Kaylee needed to be safe.

Wendy would protect her daughter at all costs.

Chapter Twenty-Eight

Ariana started to relax. Several quiet minutes had passed. No scraping, and no questions.

The pantry felt smaller with Wendy's accusation hanging between them. It felt tight and airless, as if the walls had moved in closer.

Ariana's heartbeat thudded painfully in her throat. Her stomach rumbled, but she didn't have an appetite. She grabbed some packaged items and stuffed them into her pockets for later.

Kaylee clung to her mother like a frightened shadow, eyes wide and trembling.

Wendy returned her attention to Ariana. "What are you hiding?"

Ariana opened her mouth. She needed to tread carefully. It was a delicate balance of trying to calm Wendy down, protect Damon, protect their baby, and keep the group together. But the words tangled in her chest.

"It's complicated," Ariana finally said.

"Everything is complicated. Try me."

Ariana stepped closer, hands slightly raised in a peace-offering gesture. "We're scared too. Damon's struggling with some traumatic memories. Things from his past—that's all I meant. There's no conspiracy. No secret agenda, I promise. We're all on the same team."

It wasn't a lie. It just wasn't the whole truth.

Wendy's eyes narrowed. "Memories of what?"

Before Ariana could respond, Marlene jumped in like a drowning woman clinging to the nearest floating object. "He probably knew someone like Cal Jones. Lots of people recognize famous cases. Cal's crimes were all over the news. He was terrifying."

Wendy shot Marlene a sharp look. "You're really eager to change the subject."

Marlene flinched. "I just meant, why assume Damon is involved?"

She wasn't wrong. But Ariana heard the shaky undercurrent. Marlene seemed grateful attention had shifted off her, off her connection to the hospital and Cal's family. Grateful and terrified. But why?

Wendy lifted her chin. "If Damon isn't involved, then why keep whispering? Why talk behind everyone's backs?"

Ariana tried to think of a good reply. "Because he's not doing well. And I'm trying to keep him steady."

"So talk to me. I'm not the enemy."

Ariana nodded. "Then let's keep each other close. Safe. We can talk more once we have shelter for the night."

"What about the pantry?" Kaylee asked.

Wendy looked confused. "What about it?"

"We could sleep in there. It should be big enough for everyone, and it has food. Plus, there aren't any windows that could get broken."

It wasn't the worst idea Ariana had heard. Not to mention there was likely to be a bathroom nearby.

Wendy blinked. "There aren't any blankets in there."

Marlene shrugged. "That's easy enough. We can grab some from the laundry room. It isn't too far from here."

Kaylee grimaced. "They're not dirty are they?"

"I'm sure there are clean loads there. If not, we can raid some patient rooms. The pantry's actually a good idea."

She and Kaylee exchanged a brief smile.

Wendy started to say something, but a sharp metallic drag cut her off.

This time it sounded closer.

Like something heavy sliding across the floor just beyond the kitchen door.

Kaylee whimpered and immediately moved closer to Wendy. "Mom!"

Wendy clutched her tighter, eyes darting toward the hallway. "What *was* that?"

Ariana grabbed Wendy's free arm, squeezing. "Stay close. Everyone stay close."

Marlene pressed herself to the pantry shelves, trembling hard enough to rattle the canned goods. "That... that wasn't wind."

The dragging sound came again. Slow, deliberate, and scraping along tile.

Ariana's pulse spiked painfully.

Wendy whispered, "It's getting closer."

"We can't stay boxed in here. We need to move to open space."

"But that's toward the hall!" Wendy's voice cracked.

"We can't let whoever that is corner us." Ariana grabbed a heavy mixing bowl from a shelf—anything to use as a makeshift weapon. "Stay behind me."

Wendy, eyes wet, pulled Kaylee behind her. She stood tall, terrified but resolute. "Okay, okay."

Marlene clutched her keys. "Maybe it's... maybe it's an animal."

"It's not," Ariana whispered.

The sound wasn't just dragging, but a faint, rhythmic sound beneath it.

Footsteps.

Coming directly toward them.

The hallway lights flickered.

The dragging stopped.

Silence.

Ariana's breath trembled.

Kaylee whimpered. Wendy rubbed her hair.

Marlene's teeth chattered audibly.

Then a soft, unmistakable creak.

The kitchen door opening.

Ariana lifted the bowl, heart hammering in her throat.

"We move," she whispered. "Now."

All questions forgotten. Secrets kept safely hidden.

Fear the only thing shared between them.

They braced themselves as the noise grew louder from whatever waited on the other side.

Chapter Twenty-Nine

Ariana tightened her grip on the metal mixing bowl, muscles coiled, breath shallow.

Kaylee hid behind Wendy, wielding a wooden spoon.

Wendy pressed one hand to Kaylee's head and the other to Ariana's shoulder, steady but trembling.

Marlene stood rigid, clutching her keys like she meant to stab someone with them. "I don't... I don't know what that noise is." Her voice cracked. "Nobody's supposed to be here."

Kaylee held the spoon higher. "Maybe it's the guys?"

Ariana narrowed her eyes at the faint sliver of darkness visible through the cracked door. "They wouldn't make that same dragging noise that we heard before..." She didn't want to say 'before Lana died.'

Wendy drew in a deep breath. "We better do this."

"I'm scared," Kaylee said.

"Then stay back." Wendy made eye contact with Ariana and Marlene. "On three."

Ariana nodded, ready. If needed, all of her personal safety training would kick in automatically.

Marlene shuddered. "Fine."

"Mom..." Kaylee gulped.

Wendy kissed the top of her head. "Stay back, sweetheart."

The dragging sound came again. Closer now, scraping against tile, metal on stone.

Ariana muttered under her breath.

Wendy took a step forward. "One..."

The lights above them flickered.

"Two..."

Something in the hallway creaked like it was shifting its weight.

Ariana breathed in, steadying her pulse.

"Three!"

Wendy shoved the kitchen door fully open.

It banged against the wall.

A figure jerked upright from behind one of the prep counters.

It was a man.

Ariana froze.

He was unshaven, pale from cold, wearing a thin medical scrub top beneath a heavy coat. His eyes were sunken, darting fast between the three women like a cornered animal.

Kaylee screamed.

Wendy jumped in front of her.

Ariana swung the mixing bowl toward his head.

But the man lifted both hands quickly. "Wait! Please! Marlene?"

Ariana froze mid-strike, breath catching.

Marlene gasped. "Ed?"

The man sagged with relief, hand over his heart. "Thank God. I thought... I thought you were someone else."

"Same." Marlene sucked in ragged breaths.

Ariana didn't lower the bowl. Not yet. "Who are you?"

Ed's gaze flitted around the room nervously. "I worked here. Came here when the power in my cabin went out. I heard doors shutting and footsteps. Someone dragging things around."

"That was you!" Wendy snapped.

Ed shook his head vigorously. "No, I was hiding. I've been hiding since the storm hit."

Ariana exchanged a look with Wendy. She looked as uneasy as Ari felt.

Marlene stepped forward, voice trembling but soft. "This is Ed Thompson. He used to work in the old psych wing. Maintenance tech."

Ed nodded without taking his eyes off the doorway behind them. "I live off-grid a few miles north. When I got here, I noticed the roof had a weak support beam. Had to reinforce it, then the wind knocked out the power and the emergency lights came on and..." His breathing shuttered. "Then someone started moving around inside."

Wendy pulled Kaylee closer. "You're saying you weren't alone?"

Ed's jaw tightened. "Not even before the storm hit."

A cold ripple ran down Ariana's spine. "And you didn't shatter the window in the break room?"

"Why would I do that?"

"Somebody did."

Kaylee stepped to her mom's side. "It could've just been the storm."

"Not with the wristband being thrown inside. And who's been making the noises?" Wendy asked.

Ed's expression twisted. From fear? Exhaustion? "I don't know. I haven't seen anyone else. But they've been down here with me. Moving through the rooms. Leaving things where they don't belong."

Ariana held her breath.

The dragging sound, the lights flickering.

Staged clues. Lana's last screams.

Wendy's voice dropped to a trembling whisper. "Did you see a young woman?"

Ed's face fell. "I heard her. Earlier. She was screaming for help. Unfortunately, I couldn't get to her in time."

Marlene covered her mouth with both hands.

Ariana's heart plummeted. "You didn't go to her when she was crying out?"

"I tried." Shame flashed across Ed's face. "But she stopped screaming. And then... whoever else is in here started coming toward me. I heard the footsteps."

Ariana's legs almost buckled.

Someone else was here. Hunting.

How many people were in this abandoned hospital?

Kaylee sniffled but kept her head high.

Ariana reached for Wendy's arm. "We need to get back to the guys. Now."

"There are others?" Ed looked around.

Marlene nodded. "Three men. We all heard the noises down in the basement. They went to check it out while we came to scavenge food."

Ed glanced toward the pantry. "Isn't much in there. Supply's been dwindling for some time."

Wendy arched an eyebrow. "You've been tracking it?"

"Yeah." He said it like it was the most normal thing.

Ariana's pulse spiked. If both Marlene and Ed came back here since the hospital shut down, then that meant others probably did too.

Including someone obsessed with Cal Jones.

How long would she and Damon be able to keep the secret of their relation to him?

And would the group still accept them once they found out?

Chapter Thirty

Damon stiffened as he heard an out of place sound. Reed and Eric didn't appear to notice.

A sharp bang, followed by a scuffling echo that rolled down the basement corridor from the direction of the kitchen wing.

They were getting closer to Ariana and the others. It felt like they'd been following the signs for hours, but had to be less than fifteen minutes.

Time didn't move at the normal pace here in the hospital.

Another bang.

Reed stopped. "Did you hear that?"

"Yeah." Damon's stomach twisted. Was Ariana safe?

Eric looked around. "I didn't hear anything."

"We need to hurry." Damon rushed ahead.

Reed didn't argue this time. His flashlight beam jerked wildly across the concrete as they sprinted down the hall, boots smacking through cold pools of air and scattered papers.

Eric stayed close behind, muttering under his breath.

The storm above groaned through ducts. The building itself felt like it was suffocating.

Damon didn't slow. "Ari! Wendy! Kaylee!"

His voice echoed back at him, loud and empty.

The men reached another stairwell. Damon bounded up first, taking the steps two at a time. Reed cursed behind him to slow down, but Damon didn't. Couldn't.

Ariana was up there. Pregnant and probably terrified.

His chest tightened until breathing hurt.

When they reached the wing with the kitchen, the hallway looked wrong. Too dark, too quiet. Shouldn't they hear the women's conversation?

Damon held up his flashlight, its weak beam cutting through the gloom.

Reed froze mid-step. "What the...?"

Damon followed the angle of Reed's trembling finger.

Something was propped against the wall outside the kitchen doors.

Human-shaped. Head bowed.

For a sickening heartbeat he thought it was a real body.

Then the beam hit plastic skin.

A CPR mannequin. Propped upright like someone had posed it intentionally.

Eric gagged. "You've got to be kidding me."

But it wasn't the mannequin's presence that made Damon's blood run cold.

It was the staging.

The dummy lay slumped with its head against the wall, fake limbs positioned perfectly, arms folded across its chest. A red marker was smeared across its torso—deliberate strokes forming jagged lines.

Reed's breath hitched. "Is that—?"

Damon's entire body locked.

It was a recreation. Another one.

A crude but unmistakable mimicry of one of Cal's killings.

The one where he left a woman posed, head tilted against a basement wall, red paint across her chest proclaiming "there will be more."

His father's words, repeated in every article Damon ever tried to burn.

Eric stumbled backward. "Who would... who'd do this?"

Reed threw Damon a harsh glance. He had to recognize the staging too.

Damon's pulse hammered hard and fast, heat flashing through his limbs. He stepped closer despite every cell in his body screaming at him not to. As he approached, his flashlight caught a piece of paper tucked under the mannequin's stiff plastic fingers.

Folded neatly.

Waiting.

His name scrawled across the front in jagged marker.

Damon.

Reed swore. "We need to remove you and your wife from our group! You're going to get the rest of us killed."

"You'd leave my pregnant wife stranded?"

"Better her than me."

Red hot fury ran through Damon, but then the note with his name on it rushed over him like an icy river.

His hands shook as he pulled the note free.

Inside was a single sentence written in thick, uneven strokes.

Like father, like son.

Damon's knees wobbled.

The walls pressed inward, the air thinned, and the buzz in his skull grew into a full-body roar.

Eric's eyes widened. "What does *that* mean?"

Reed stared at Damon like he was seeing him for the first time. "What aren't you telling us?"

Damon couldn't speak.

Not with that message on the page, not with his father's ghost crawling out of the basement walls. And definitely not with Ariana somewhere not far away, probably hearing the same noises, probably terrified.

He crushed the paper in his fist. "Someone is trying to get under my skin. What we need is to find the women and Kaylee."

But before he could take a step toward the kitchen, the lights above flickered.

Then a scream tore through the hallway.

A woman's voice. Wendy.

Damon's heart stopped.

Ariana was with her. What if something happened to her, and that was why Wendy yelled?

He ran down the hall, shoved his shoulder into the swinging door, and pushed it open with a force that startled even himself. But he didn't care.

He didn't even feel it.

All he knew was that something in the kitchen had made Wendy scream.

And he needed to protect Ariana and their unborn baby.

Chapter Thirty-One

Ariana held the bowl ready to actually use it as a weapon this time. The footsteps out in the hallway sounded like a herd of elephants. She prayed it was Damon and the others, but at this point, anything was possible. Maybe they were being chased by the killer.

Damon burst through the kitchen door. His eyes found Ariana instantly—as if nothing else in the room existed. Relief broke across his face so fiercely she felt it in her chest, a sharp ache.

Then his gaze snapped to Ed.

His relief vanished.

Reed stormed in behind him, shoving into Damon, and his flashlight pinned Ed like a spotlight.

Eric followed, panting, looking ready to flee or fight, or both. "Who in blazes is that?"

Ed lifted both hands again. "It's okay. I worked here. Maintenance. I'm not armed. I'm not—"

"You expect us to believe that?" Reed barked, stepping

forward. "You were hiding in the kitchen? Stalking around the halls? Dragging things on the floor?"

Ed flinched. "It wasn't me. Who are you?"

Marlene stood at Ed's side. "He really did work here. We can trust him."

Reed didn't take his gaze from Ed. "Tell us yourself! Who are you?"

Wendy stepped in front of him, eyes blazing. "Stop shouting at him! He scared us, but he didn't hurt us."

Reed whirled on her. "We just found a staged murder scene down the hall and you want to defend some creep lurking in the dark?"

Ariana stiffened. "Murder scene?"

Kaylee whimpered. "Someone else died?"

Wendy pulled her daughter to the side. "That's it. We're taking our chances with the storm in our car."

Eric glared at her. "We're not going anywhere."

"You can stay here with a murderer and dead bodies if you want, but we're not."

Reed huffed. "It wasn't an actual murder. I said *staged*."

Ariana reeled with confusion. "Staged with what?"

"A CPR dummy."

Eric frowned at his wife. "See? No reason to leave."

"Right. Someone only sent a message that they plan to kill one of us after two people have already been murdered. Nothing to worry about."

As they stared each other down, Ariana's attention went back to her husband.

Damon still hadn't spoken since returning. He stood motionless, chest rising and falling quickly, fists clenched at his sides.

Ariana grabbed his arm gently. "Everyone's okay."

He nodded but didn't look away from Ed.

Reed moved closer to Ed. "Start talking. All of it. Now. If you want my trust, you're going to have to earn it."

Ed drew in a deep breath. "I came here when the storm took out power at my place, which isn't far from here. I do off-grid work... building repairs, storm prep. The hospital was deteriorating even before it got shut down. Some of us come by to do upkeep here and there, you know, to keep out vandals." He wiped his hands on his coat. "Then the storm hit. I got stuck inside."

"And the noises?" Eric demanded.

Ed's expression twisted. "Those weren't me."

"Convenient," Reed snapped.

Ariana stepped forward, putting herself slightly between Reed and Ed. "Did you see anyone else? Another person? A woman? A man?"

Ed shook his head. "Only heard them. Moving. Dragging things. Opening doors and not closing them again. I tried to avoid them."

"So you ran," Reed accused.

"Yes! I ran. Because whoever is down there isn't normal."

Silence stretched across the room.

Marlene stepped forward timidly. "Are you saying you think it's a former patient? From the psych ward?"

Reed snorted. "So now we're supposed to trust you again?"

Marlene shot him an annoyed glance.

Wendy folded her arms, stepping beside Ariana now, like they'd formed a silent alliance. "We're not getting anywhere pointing fingers at random."

"That's funny," Reed said sharply, "coming from the woman who thinks Marlene's involved."

Marlene whipped her head to Wendy.

She flushed. "I didn't say you were involved. You're all

strangers, and I can't blindly trust anyone. Not with my daughter here."

Damon finally spoke. "Unless she separated from you all, she couldn't have set up that scene. You wouldn't have been able to miss it before you came into the kitchen."

The room fell dead quiet at his voice.

A chill ran down Ariana's spine. Someone had set up a fake murder scene while they were in the kitchen.

Reed huffed. "Might as well tell them about the picture and the note."

Damon reached into his coat pocket without a word and pulled out the crumpled note, smoothing it open on the counter.

Ariana felt Damon tense, and she stood closer to him.

Reed tapped the paper. "A staged murder, posed exactly like the Cal Jones copycat killing. And this—" he pointed at the jagged handwriting "—was left for Damon."

Wendy's face drained of color. "Why Damon?"

Ariana's breath caught.

Damon stared at the floor, silent and trembling.

Her heart ached for him, and her mind raced for a way to protect him from having to expose the truth.

Reed's eyes sharpened.

Ariana stepped between them. "Stop. He's a victim too—"

"Of what?" Reed demanded. "If this is connected to Cal Jones, why him?"

Ariana's stomach twisted. She felt Damon flinch behind her.

He wasn't ready for this.

None of them were.

Ed's eyes went wide. "Cal Jones? *The* Cal Jones? What am I missing?"

Marlene nodded shakily. "He was here for assessments years ago."

Ed cursed under his breath. "No one told me that."

Kaylee moved closer to her dad.

He rubbed his temples. "What is happening to us?"

Reed dropped his flashlight on the counter. "Look, someone here is lying. And Damon—Cal's *son*—is the one getting personal messages from a killer. We deserve to know why."

Wendy's eyes widened. "What?"

Marlene stepped closer to Damon. "I *knew* there was something familiar about you."

A sharp metallic bang echoed from out in the hallway.

Everyone froze.

"That's the noise I told you about." Ed's face drained of color. "That's what I heard before."

Ariana grabbed Damon's hand.

Wendy pulled Kaylee close.

Marlene backed toward the wall.

Reed raised his flashlight like a weapon.

Eric stepped behind him.

Another bang. This time closer.

This time, followed by the slow, unmistakable drag of something heavy across the tile.

Ariana's blood ran cold.

Damon squeezed her hand, voice barely audible. "He's not done with us yet."

Chapter Thirty-Two

Wendy didn't want to follow the sound. She didn't want to walk deeper into the wing, with its flickering lights and the sickening drag of something heavy scraping tile just beyond their sight.

But Kaylee clung to her, trembling, and Wendy wasn't letting her out of arm's reach—not now. Not ever again if she could help it.

Reed had already pushed forward, Damon close behind him, flashlight beams slicing through the hallway. Eric followed reluctantly. Marlene stuck near the back, muttering reassurances that convinced absolutely no one. Ed shuffled somewhere in the middle, jumpy as a stray cat.

Ariana walked beside Wendy, one hand lightly placed on her shoulder, the other held tight at her belly, protecting the life growing there. Wendy couldn't help but soften a little at that. Fear made them all sharp and wild, but that baby made Ariana something different.

Still, Wendy hadn't forgotten the unanswered questions.

They rounded another counter, stepping through the

shadows toward the walk-in freezer area. The dragging had stopped, replaced now by a soft tapping. It didn't sound like something natural to the building.

Reed held up his flashlight. "It's coming from there."

Wendy's grip tightened on Kaylee's arm. "Behind the freezer door?"

Eric swallowed. "No way. I'm not opening that."

Ariana stepped forward suddenly. "Wait, look."

A piece of paper stuck out from beneath the freezer door, caught under the metal threshold as though someone slid it from inside.

Wendy's pulse hammered.

Everyone stared, but Reed crouched and plucked it up. "*Another* message?"

Ariana reached for it before he could unfold it. Her face tightened, jaw clenched. Something inside her braced for what the note would reveal. Ariana unfolded it with careful fingers.

Wendy leaned over to see.

The handwriting was jagged and uneven.

Different from the message left for Damon, but no less chilling.

You should have left when you had the chance. The snow won't save you. Not this time, Ariana.

Wendy's stomach plummeted.

"Ari..." Damon's voice cracked. He took a step toward her, eyes wide with panic.

Wendy's own fear spiked. "Why is someone talking to *you* specifically?"

Ariana stiffened, but she didn't answer. She just stared at the note, frozen and pale.

Marlene backed away from the freezer. "Someone's in there. Someone must be. Slide a note from inside..."

Reed reached for the freezer latch.

"No!" Wendy reached to stop him. "We don't know what's behind that door."

Kaylee whimpered. Wendy pulled her closer.

Ed whispered, "This is bad. This is worse than anything I've seen here."

Wendy's mind raced. Someone knew Ariana's name.

Someone had written to *her*. Someone had followed them or had been waiting for them.

Because she was married to Cal Jones's son?

"How do they know you?" Wendy demanded. Fear sharpened her voice into something unforgiving. "Ariana, what aren't you telling us?"

A sudden bang. It sounded like someone hitting metal.

Everyone jumped.

Kaylee screamed.

Marlene bumped into Eric.

Reed backed up fast, raising his flashlight like a weapon. "What was *that*?"

A second bang echoed.

Then silence.

Wendy's heart clawed up her throat. She pivoted to Ariana. "Stick close. Don't go anywhere. We need to—"

But Ariana wasn't there. She'd been standing right next to the corner of the hall. Now she was gone.

Wendy blinked hard, scanning the circle of flashlights.

"Ariana?" she called, voice tightening. "Ari?"

No answer.

Damon spun around, panic exploding across his face. "Ariana!"

Reed cursed, sweeping his flashlight across the floor, the counters, the dark corners.

Ed backed up so fast he hit the wall. "Where... where did she go?"

Wendy grabbed Kaylee tighter, chest seizing. "She was right beside me."

A soft sound drifted from deeper in the kitchen wing.

Not a bang or a drag.

A quiet, desperate cry.

Farther away, fading.

Damon's face went white. "She didn't walk away. Someone took her."

Wendy's blood ran cold.

The killer had taken her.

Chapter Thirty-Three

Damon's chest collapsed inward. His vision tunneled. Air scraped into his lungs painfully.

Ariana was gone. The world narrowed to that single, brutal truth. Not the banging freezer door. Not Reed shouting orders. Not Wendy panicking or the others scattering flashlights across the kitchen like frantic fireflies.

His wife wasn't here. All because he'd been so wrapped up in himself. If he'd have been sharper, he could have prevented this.

It was all his fault. Now it was on him to make it right.

He yelled her name so loud it scraped his throat raw. "Ariana!"

He spun toward the hallway. Empty.

The pantry. Empty.

Everything was empty of her—except for the faint echo of footsteps that might've been real or imagined.

His pulse roared in his ears. The kitchen walls pressed closer and closer, every stainless-steel surface reflecting the panic in his eyes, the panic he tried his whole life to hide.

Reed grabbed his arm. "Damon! Hey, stop. You have to breathe, man."

Damon shoved him off with more force than intended.

Reed stumbled into the counter.

"Don't touch me," Damon snapped, voice cracking under the weight of terror. "I have to find her. I have to!"

Horrible images slammed into him. Ariana tied to a chair. Crying for him. Bleeding. Motionless.

Damon shook. His thoughts crashing like waves during a storm he couldn't out swim. He felt old rage, old violence clawing up his throat. The same darkness he'd spent his life trying to bury after years living with an unpredictable and cruel father.

If he didn't get control, he would lose himself.

And he couldn't lose himself.

Not when Ari needed him more than ever. He couldn't protect his mom, but he would save his wife.

"Damon," Eric said quietly, stepping between him and the others. "Look at me."

He didn't want to, couldn't. But Eric's voice was steady.

"Don't let this break you," Eric said. "Ariana wouldn't want that."

Ariana.

Damon squeezed his eyes shut, forcing a shuddering breath into his lungs.

She needed him.

He repeated it—mentally, fiercely, until his heart obeyed. *Ariana needs you.* Then he inhaled again. Held the breath. Exhaled through clenched teeth.

The spiral didn't vanish, but the world came back into focus through the haze.

Damon straightened slowly, still trembling and hollowed out, but most importantly, in control.

Wendy watched him with wet, fearful eyes. "We have to find her. Damon... you know she wouldn't just leave."

Damon shoved the ache threatening to break him all over again. "I know."

Reed cleared his throat, uncomfortable with emotion but aware they needed direction. "Whoever took her didn't get far. We heard the struggle. The note was meant to lure her closer."

Ed added, "The killer might know this place as well as Marlene and I do. They'll use the hidden areas."

She nodded frantically. "The tunnels and old seclusion rooms. Maybe even the generator rooms. There are dozens of places someone could hide."

Each word stabbed Damon through the ribs.

"She's strong," Wendy said firmly, voice breaking. "She'll fight and win. We have to believe that."

Damon turned toward the hallway, posture tightening with purpose. Not rage or panic, and definitely not the inherited violence he feared lurked in his blood. But determination. "She *is* alive, and I'm going to get her back." He clenched the note for her in his fist. His jaw set like steel. "You made a mistake. A fatal one."

Reed frowned. "What mistake?"

Damon looked down the corridor where Ariana had vanished and let out a breath that felt like the beginning of a war. "He took the one person I would burn this place down to save."

And he started forward into the dark, into the unknown, and into the jaws of the nightmare he'd outrun his whole life.

Only one thought consumed him—he wasn't stopping until Ariana was in his arms again.

Chapter Thirty-Four

Wendy couldn't stop shaking. It was all too much. This weekend was supposed to be one last idyllic holiday for Kaylee before serving Eric with the divorce papers. Of course it ended up so spectacularly the opposite. Getting stranded from the storm, bodies piling up, running from a killer.

Now the other mom in the group was missing after the other young women was killed. No one was safe.

Everyone was arguing about what to do next. Damon was ready to run off on his own, but Reed, Eric, and Marlene blocked him from being able to get away. They insisted everyone stay together, despite how large the group had grown.

And shrunk.

Wendy's thoughts spun out of control. Lana's body. The mystery body. Damon was the son of Cal Jones.

He could be more dangerous than the rest of them. Murder ran through his blood, his very DNA.

Maybe that was the real reason the others were blocking him from leaving.

Damon defended himself. "I was with you all when the murders took place! You can't seriously think I had anything to do with any of this. Move aside so I can save my wife. If anything happens to her, you're all to blame!"

Marlene's voice cut through the air. "What's this?"

Wendy's heart sunk. She hadn't found another body, had she?

Damon moved past those blocking him, determination burning in his eyes. "What is it?"

Marlene held up a note. Another one.

"Where did you find that?" Reed demanded.

"It was on the ground where Ariana was last standing."

Reed's eyes narrowed. "Liar."

"Excuse me?" Marlene put her hands to her hips.

"Why did *you* find it?"

"Because I saw it."

Reed marched directly in front of her. "How convenient."

Ed stepped closer to them and looked at Reed. "What are you accusing her of?"

"Planting the note. Maybe she wrote all of them." He turned his attention back to Marlene. "Let's see your handwriting."

"Why?"

"To make sure you aren't the author of the notes."

She shoved him, then backed away. "I don't owe you anything. We need to find Ariana, and we need to see what this note says."

"Exactly what the killer would say."

Ed glared at him. "Lay off."

"Or what, old man?"

"You want all of us to turn on you?" Ed snapped. "We will."

"Why are you so defensive of Marlene?"

"Because I know her. She wouldn't hurt a fly."

Reed snorted.

"Stop!" Damon grabbed the note from Marlene and shot a threatening look at Reed. "The *only* thing that matters is finding my pregnant wife."

Ed's mouth fell open.

Wendy drew in a deep breath and stood defensively in front of Kaylee, who was as pale as a ghost. "Read the note."

Damon held it up.

Wendy's knees turned to rubber.

On the outside of the folded note was one word.

Eric.

Reed muttered, "You've got to be kidding me."

Eric's face drained of color. "No... no, that's not possible. Why me?"

Wendy grabbed Eric's wrist. "Don't touch it."

But he did. Then he opened the note.

Her husband crumbled. "No, not now. Not here."

"What does it say?" Reed demanded, stepping closer.

Eric's eyes filled with fear. He opened his mouth, but no words came out.

Marlene grabbed the note. "It says, 'I didn't forget you. Debts don't die. —Cal.'"

Wendy couldn't breathe. There was no way she heard that right. "Cal?" she choked out.

Eric's hands shook so badly, the paper fell from his fingers then drifted to the tile. "Wendy, I didn't know how to tell you."

"Tell me *what*?" Her voice broke. "What connection could you possibly have to him?"

He sank to the floor, head in his hands. "I was almost one of his victims."

The room went silent. Even the storm outside seemed to hush.

Wendy's heart pounded.

Kaylee grabbed her arm.

Eric lifted his head, tears streaking through dust on his cheeks. "When I was sixteen... he took me. Grabbed me after school. Had me in the back of his car."

Wendy felt the world tilting. "Eric... why... didn't you ever tell me that?"

"Because he *didn't* kill me." Eric's voice cracked, raw and strangled. "Cal changed his mind. He said... said I could be useful, so he let me go, but only if I... helped him. Reported things. Covered tracks. Stole stuff from the church charity I volunteered at. He said if I ever told anyone, he'd kill me. And my family."

Wendy's jaw dropped. "You *worked* for him?"

"I was just a kid," Eric said, sobbing now. "A *scared* kid. I didn't know what I was doing."

"You covered for a murderer!" Wendy leaned against the wall, unable to support herself. "Even a sixteen-year-old knows that much."

"He threatened my parents and sister!"

Reed pulled on his hair. "And you didn't mention *any of this* while we're being hunted by someone reenacting Cal's murders?"

Wendy couldn't breathe. As she stared at her husband, she saw a stranger. She'd known about the affairs, but she'd never dreamed he was hiding anything like this. "You lied to me. For our entire marriage. You lied!"

"I tried to bury it," Eric sobbed. "When Cal was arrested, I thought it was over. I thought he was gone and it was done. But someone found out. Someone here knows."

Reed let out an incredulous bark of laughter. "What the hell is going on? Is *everyone* here connected to Cal Jones somehow?" His eyes darted between Damon and Eric, then to everyone else. "Better let us know now. If anything else comes out after this—after lying now—you'll be kicked from the group. No questions asked."

Nobody said anything.

Reed threw his hands in the air. "Am I the only one here who didn't share a childhood with a serial killer?"

Wendy barely heard him. Her heart felt like it was splitting open.

Because Eric, who she'd spent the last two decades with, who was the father of her child, had been living under the shadow of a monster.

And he'd never told her.

She knelt slowly, looking him straight in the eyes. "Did Cal ever hurt you?"

Eric closed his eyes. "He didn't have to."

Anger roiled through Wendy. She wanted to scream. To shake him and demand every detail he'd hidden from her.

But Kaylee's hand tightened around hers.

Ariana was still missing.

And a killer was still in these walls.

So Wendy shoved aside her heartbreak and stood again. "We'll deal with this later." Her voice shook but remained firm. "Right now, we need to find Ariana."

Reed's brows furrowed. "Your husband could be the killer!"

"Then we make sure he doesn't leave our sight."

Everyone nodded in agreement.

Chapter Thirty-Five

Damon moved fast. Too fast for the rest of the group, but he wouldn't slow down. Nothing would stop him. Couldn't think without seeing Ariana gone, taken, terrified somewhere in the dark.

He whispered her name under his breath. "Ariana... Ariana... I'm coming, Ari..."

Eric's revelation rattled inside Damon's skull like a loose bolt in a machine about to fall apart.

Eric had known Cal. Been taken by him. Manipulated, threatened. Used.

Damon's stomach twisted.

The coincidence was too much. Someone had brought Damon here. And Eric. Knowing the histories they themselves didn't even know they shared.

This wasn't random. It was orchestrated. That was the only explanation.

Reed stomped beside him, muttering curses. "We're losing time. We should split up."

"No," Damon snapped. "No splitting up."

Everyone fell silent.

Ed huddled behind them, arms shaking. "The hall to the right leads to old pediatrics... the left goes to the psych wing."

Damon's breath hitched. Psych wing.

"Where would they take Ariana?" Wendy whispered, hugging Kaylee close. "Where would she be safest?"

"Nowhere," Reed said bluntly. "There is no safe here."

Damon felt something feral rise in him.

Wendy shuddered. "This is all too much to be a coincidence. Three people connected to Cal? Eric, Damon, and Marlene. But how? Why now?"

Damon turned, eyes narrowing. "What brought you two out here? Why were you on this road?"

Wendy blinked, confused. "We were on our way to my parents' for Christmas. Just a normal, happy holiday..." She hesitated.

"You're hiding something." Damon straightened his shoulders.

Wendy nodded before glancing over at her husband. "No point in keeping it a secret any longer. It was supposed to be one last family memory... before I served Eric with divorce papers."

Kaylee gasped and moved away from her. "Mom! How could you?"

Wendy started to say something, but Kaylee turned her back to her. Wendy's face fell, but she didn't say anything.

Eric squirmed but said nothing.

Marlene coughed awkwardly.

Damon pressed, voice harsh with urgency. "Where were you heading before the drive?"

Wendy frowned. "We were going to the Maple Oak Lodge. They sent us some holiday deals. They gave us a discount code. The lodge was offering huge promotions this season."

Damon's breath hitched. "That's where Ariana and I were booked. They not only emailed us offers but sent several mailings to the house."

Wendy nodded. "Us too. I just thought it was a heavy-handed advertising campaign. Even someone I knew was pushing me to go. She said our family needed it."

"Who's she?" Reed demanded.

"I only know her by her screenname." Wendy frowned.

"Which is?"

"Hotmama34."

Reed's brows drew together. "That's all you know about your friend?"

"Yes!" Wendy said. "It's an online forum."

Damon's mind raced. "Now it's obvious we were targeted by the same promotion."

Eric's face paled. "Wait. You two had the same discount?"

Damon raked his hands through his hair. "Ariana signed us up because she said it felt... meant to be." His voice broke. "A romantic weekend together after a rough year."

Reed swore loudly. "So let me get this straight—you all got pulled to the same lodge? With the same discount code? From someone you barely know?"

Wendy stiffened. "She was an acquaintance from my parenting group."

The lights cut out.

Total darkness.

Kaylee screamed.

Ed dropped his flashlight and cursed.

Reed shouted for everyone to stay where they were.

For one horrifying second, Damon couldn't see anything—not the group, the walls, or even his own hands.

Then the flashlights flicked on one by one. Harsh, swinging beams slicing the dark.

Wendy's face was white with terror.

Kaylee leaned against her.

Reed's gaze bounced around the room.

Eric trembled, clutching the note with white knuckles.

Ed backed into the wall, muttering.

Damon lifted his flashlight, breath caught in his throat. "Where's Marlene?"

Silence.

He swept the hall with the light. It was only empty tile stretching into blackness.

"Marlene!" Wendy shouted.

Eric spun in a circle. "She was right behind us."

Reed cursed. "Did she just wander off again?"

The hair on the back of Damon's neck rose.

Had she wandered off? Or had she been taken?

Just like Ariana.

He tightened his grip on the flashlight until his fingers hurt. "Ariana has a connection to Cal. Marlene met him. Now they're both gone."

"Everyone stay together," Reed said, voice low and cracking with rage. "Nobody else disappears."

Damon stepped forward into the darkness. "We need to find Ariana. Now."

"And Marlene," Kaylee whispered. "Are they going to try and take Dad too?"

"No," Wendy said quickly.

"You don't know that."

The kid had her there.

Damon turned to the girl. "If he stays close to the group, he'll be fine. Just like everyone else."

He hoped.

Chapter Thirty-Six

Ariana shivered, waking slowly with a pounding headache. The flat, biting cold pressed straight through her clothes, straight through her skin, straight into bone. The darkness was so complete she couldn't tell if her eyes were open at all. Breath hitching, she instinctively reached for her stomach, for her baby. Thankfully, her hands were free.

She felt the sore spot near her right temple. A goose egg was already forming.

When she tried to sit up, something metal jerked tight around her ankle.

Panic surged through her like a current.

She scrambled backward, but it held fast, scraping against concrete. Her fingers found the cuff locked around her right ankle, cold and rigid. She tugged hard, her efforts painful, useless.

She wasn't going anywhere.

Ariana sucked in a breath, forcing herself to still. "Okay, okay. Breathe."

The air tasted stale. Dusty. Like a forgotten storage room or a sealed basement cell.

She pressed a hand outward, searching.

A wall only a foot away.

Cold tile beneath her palms.

Something metallic beside her knee. Maybe an overturned tray or stool.

The room was small. Really small.

"Damon," she whispered.

Her head throbbed, the pain growing stronger. She didn't remember losing consciousness. One moment she'd been in the kitchen wing, stepping back from the freezer door to get some air as nausea hit. The next, something pressed at her back.

That was when she was struck.

Ariana shuddered.

She forced herself upright, inching along the floor until her back hit the far wall. The restraint clinked softly. The darkness pressed in, heavy and smothering.

"Okay," she murmured to the baby, voice trembling. "We're okay. I'm going to make sure we get through this."

A faint humming vibrated somewhere above her. Old electrical wires or a failing generator. Pipes clanged far in the distance.

Then footsteps.

Slow, steady, deliberate.

Just like the ones she'd heard before.

Ariana froze.

They stopped just outside the door.

She didn't breathe.

Metal scraped. It was the sound of something sliding into a slot or latch.

A light flickered to life overhead, so weak it barely reached the floor, turning the room a sickly yellow-green.

Ariana blinked hard against the sudden change.

The room was small, maybe eight by eight feet. Bare concrete. Rusted drain near her foot. A locked door with a tiny, covered window. It was her cell.

And on the floor in front of the door... a piece of folded paper.

Ariana crawled toward it, metal dragging behind her. Her hands shook as she picked it up.

She flipped it open.

Her breath caught in her throat.

You always come back to where it started.
Let's see if he does the same.

Her pulse pounded.

This wasn't about her.

This was about Damon.

Her kidnapper wanted him here. He wanted him searching, unraveling, suffering.

Wanted him punished.

"Damon," she whispered, throat aching. "Please don't come alone. Don't follow every breadcrumb. Please..."

Ariana felt the walls closing in again.

She squeezed the note until the paper buckled. "We're getting out. I'm not waiting for you to find me. We're getting out."

Ari scanned the room, eyes adjusting to the light.

The restraints, the cuff. A heavy locked door. The flickering light fixture, with exposed wiring at the edge.

Her mind raced.

She was strong. A fighter.

Most importantly, she had a baby to protect, a husband to return to.

And she had survived worse.

Ariana pushed herself to her feet—shaky, unsteady, but

determined. "I'm coming back to you," she whispered into the dark. "Just hold on."

The footsteps faded down the hall again.

She started testing every inch of the chain.

Every bolt in the wall, every possible weakness.

Because she wasn't staying in this room.

Not one minute longer than she had to.

Chapter Thirty-Seven

Damon moved like a man possessed. He definitely felt disconnected from his body. Everything was surreal. He'd put so much effort into keeping Cal Jones in his past.

Yet here he was, rearing his murderous head again. And now Ariana was missing and in danger.

Again.

Maybe she and the baby would be better off without him in their lives. He only brought destruction with him.

The thought shattered his heart, but that didn't make it any less real. Any less right. If he wanted to give them the best, then maybe walking away would be the highest gift he could give them.

After making sure they were safe and well.

Damon glanced back. As much as he wanted to press forward, the last thing he needed was to get separated and go missing himself.

Reed and Eric kept pace behind him, flashlights cutting erratic streaks along the decaying corridor walls. Ed followed awkwardly, jumping at every noise. Wendy stayed several steps behind with Kaylee, her fear radiating like static.

They'd gone through two hallways with nothing but old equipment. Still, Damon refused to slow, think, or feel anything except the driving need to get to his wife. "Ari! Ariana!"

Only the storm answered back.

Eric jogged to catch up. "Damon, we need a plan. Running blind isn't going to help anything."

"We're not blind," Damon snapped. "We're heading toward the secured wings. She'll be there. Somewhere hidden. Do you know where?"

"I'm as much a victim in this as you are."

"Maybe."

"You helped him too," Eric shot back. "I wasn't the only one who drew his victims to him so he was never seen publicly with them."

That hit harder anything else anyone could've said to him. Damon had originally met Ariana because Cal had sent him after her, a cop's daughter. But Damon had come to his senses.

Not that it changed the fact it was how they'd met. He *had* been doing his father's bidding.

But Ariana was safe. Cal hadn't gotten to her.

Reed broke into Damon's thoughts. "It makes sense. Psych wing had the most locked rooms. If I were the psychopath behind all this, that's where I'd—"

"Don't finish that sentence," Wendy cut in.

Kaylee caught up with Damon, slowing briefly as they passed. "We'll find her."

Damon swallowed. "Yeah. We will."

They rounded another corner, and Damon stopped so abruptly Reed crashed into him.

"Oh, my..." Wendy breathed.

Hide and Seek

There, in the middle of the hallway floor, lay a small scrap of paper.

Folded neatly.

Damon dropped to his knees so fast it hurt.

His hands trembled as he picked it up.

It was Ariana's handwriting.

Damon,

I'm alive, fighting.

Find me. But don't come al—

The last word was incomplete, as if someone had tried to stop her.

His vision blurred for a second before snapping back into a razor-sharp focus. Relief, rage, fear. Everything tangled at once.

Reed crouched beside him. "She wrote that? Is that her writing?"

"Yes," Damon whispered. "But we better hurry."

Wendy exhaled shakily. "Let's go."

Damon lifted the note to his chest, gripping it like it was the only real thing in the world. "I'm coming, Ari."

Before he could stand, a scream tore through the hallway.

Shrill. Raw. Terrified beyond anything they'd heard yet.

"Marlene. That's Marlene!" Ed stumbled backward. "I told you. Something else is here!"

Reed spun toward the branching hallway. "We go now!"

But Damon held up a hand. "No, no splitting up. We find Ariana."

Wendy pointed down the opposite corridor. "But Ariana's note. It's in the corridor going that way."

Reed shook his head violently. "We can't ignore a scream like that. Marlene's alive. She might know something. Might have seen something."

"She's not the one who's pregnant," Wendy snapped. "Ariana needs—"

"We don't know how long Ariana has!" Reed shot back. "Someone just grabbed Marlene. Maybe that someone is leading us to Ariana!"

Chaos erupted with fear in overlapping voices, flashlights shaking as hands trembled.

Damon closed his eyes for one breath.

Ariana's note burned in his palm.

He rose. "Reed, Eric, you go to Marlene," he ordered, voice hard as stone. "Wendy, Kaylee, Ed, you come with me. Ariana needs us now."

Reed balked. "Are you kidding me? This is insane! We don't split up when there's a killer around the corner."

"No time!" Damon shouted. "We don't know how long Ariana has!"

Wendy nodded fiercely. "I'm going with him."

Kaylee clung to her dad this time and whispered, "I'm with them."

Her mom's face fell, but she didn't argue.

Ed swallowed hard. "I... I'll help. I know the old layout. I know the hidden maintenance hallways. I can get you closer to the psych wing faster."

Reed threw up his hands in furious resignation. "Fine! Don't blame me if you get yourselves killed!"

Eric grabbed Reed's arm. "Come on! We've got to move."

The group fractured. Reed, Eric, Kaylee, and their flashlights sprinted toward Marlene's scream. Damon, Wendy, and Ed turned toward the path Ariana had pointed them to.

Damon took one last look at Ari's note. "Hold on, Ari. I'm coming!"

Chapter Thirty Eight

The chain around Ariana's ankle clinked again as she crouched beside the wall, breath steadying with each slow inhale. The room was too quiet now—silent except for her heartbeat and the faint hum of whatever old wiring still lived behind the walls.

Her captor had come in not long ago, masked and unrecognizable, demanding her to write a note to Damon. She'd tried to tell him not to come alone, but he'd yanked the pen from her then fled from the room.

Now she had even more reason to get out of here.

The kidnapper was trying to trap Damon. No way would she let that happen.

She pressed her palm to the cuff again. Cold, tight, and industrial. Whoever locked her here knew what they were doing.

But they didn't know *her*.

Ariana rose slowly, weight shifting as she tested the chain again. It extended two feet. Just enough for her to reach the corner beneath the flickering overhead light.

And the exposed wiring.

Good.

"Okay," she whispered, hand drifting instinctively to her abdomen. "I've got you. You're safe. We're getting out. Soon."

She stood on her toes, fingers brushing the broken fixture. One wire hung free, its copper guts visible through cracked insulation.

If she could pull the fixture down, she could use the metal housing. If she could pry a corner loose...

She grabbed the fixture with both hands and pulled.

It didn't budge.

She tugged harder.

Metal groaned.

Her pulse jumped. "Come on! Come on..."

It shifted a fraction.

Ariana braced her foot against the wall and yanked with every ounce of strength panic had gifted her.

The fixture tore half loose, dangling at an angle.

Sparks flickered, raining tiny shards of light.

She stumbled backward but caught herself.

The chain rattled against the concrete.

"Okay," she said breathlessly. "Okay, that's something."

Ari reached up and gripped the loosened metal casing. With two hands, she bent it downward, forcing the edge into a crude wedge.

A tool.

A small, fragile, and desperate one, but a tool nonetheless.

Her hands shook as she crouched at the bolt anchoring her chain to the wall. The wedge might fit.

Maybe.

She jammed it under the edge of the bolt then pushed with her shoulder.

Nothing.

She gritted her teeth, putting her whole body into the effort.

The metal screeched.

Just a millimeter.

But enough to start.

"Yes," she breathed. "Please, yes."

The bolt wiggled again, loosening.

A mixture of relief and anticipation coursed through her.

Her ankle throbbed from the pressure of the cuff digging into her skin with each movement, but she pushed through the pain. Every second counted. Every sound mattered. Her flesh would heal later.

A loud clang echoed outside the door—something metallic striking concrete.

Ariana froze.

Footsteps.

Drawing closer down the hall.

Her blood turned to ice.

No, no, no...

She shoved the metal wedge further, breath held, muscles burning.

Another footstep.

This one *right* outside her door.

Her pulse punched against her ribs.

She yanked the bolt with a final, desperate shove.

It didn't come free.

But it moved. Barely. Just enough that the chain lengthened an inch.

An inch she could use.

The footsteps stopped.

Right outside the door.

Ariana scrambled back, hiding the metal wedge beneath her leg. She forced herself to sit, to look terrified, helpless—she didn't have to pretend—her chest rising in short, panicked bursts.

The tiny slot in the door slid open with a metallic scrape.

Just enough for an eye to look through.

Ariana held her breath.

Held still. Held onto hope.

A single eye stared at her through the slot.

Unblinking.

Watching.

Measuring.

She felt the weight of that gaze like a hand around her throat.

Then the slot shut.

The footsteps retreated.

Slowly.

Ariana waited until they were gone. Waited until her breath could move again, until the tremor in her limbs quieted.

She pulled the metal wedge back out.

She wasn't giving up.

Not when Damon was out there searching for her.

After having read her note.

Not when someone wanted them both trapped.

She angled the wedge at the bolt again.

"We're getting out," she whispered through clenched teeth. "I swear it. We are getting out."

And she started again.

Chapter Thirty-Nine

Damon didn't tell the others he was splitting off. He just... did it.

Something sharp and instinctive pulled him down a branching corridor. It was an old emergency exit hallway with peeling paint and a dead-end sign that was obviously a lie. He could feel Ariana's fear like a pulse under his skin, tugging him forward.

"Damon!" Wendy called from around the corner. "Where are you?"

He didn't look back. Didn't say anything.

The killer wanted him. If the clues were meant for him, then he had to face it. Alone. Away from everyone else. Away from anyone the monster could use as leverage. This was his fight.

He held Ariana's note tight in his hand as he pushed deeper into the dark.

"Ari..." he whispered. "Hold on a little longer."

A scrape echoed behind him.

Then another.

He froze.

A shape peeled from the shadows near an abandoned nurses' station—a tall silhouette, hooded, deliberate, confident.

Damon's flashlight beam hit the figure's chest first. A dark coat, worn gloves, heavy boots, and then rose to the face.

A mask. White. Featureless. Like a blank human mold, smooth except for two carved-out eyeholes.

Damon's pulse punched at his ribs.

"Where is she?" He stepped forward. "Where is Ariana?"

The masked man tilted his head slightly, as if amused. A soft, creepy laugh escaped.

"I knew you'd come alone," the voice said. "Just like your father would've."

Damon's breath seized. "Don't talk about him."

"Oh, but that's why you're here." The man leaned against the counter casually, like they were old friends meeting for coffee. "That's why all of this is happening. You. The son."

Damon's muscles locked tight. "Tell me where she is."

"I will." He shrugged lazily. "After you listen."

Damon took another step. "I'm not negotiating."

"You should be, because every second you waste getting angry instead of listening… someone else stops breathing."

The threat hit Damon like a blow.

He forced himself still.

The masked man let the silence stretch before speaking again.

"I want you," he said simply. "With me."

Damon felt the floor sway beneath him. "What?"

"You heard me." The figure straightened. "Cal Jones had an empire with loyal followers, a structure, and a purpose. You know that better than anyone."

Damon shook his head slowly. "Are you crazy?"

"I'm a man on a mission. Cal's mission."

"He's dead."

"Oh, Cal is dead, but what he built? What he taught?" He spread his gloved hands. "I'm rebuilding it."

Damon's skin crawled. The man *was* crazy. "Don't do this."

The masked man stepped closer. "I want you at my side. It's in your blood. In your instincts. Don't pretend you haven't felt it. The rage, the urges, and the darkness. It's in your DNA."

Damon's throat tightened, breath coming short. "You don't know me. I was raised by my mom. It's her influence that I live by."

The killer laughed. "I know everything about you. I've been following you for months. You live in that gated community in Rosy Hills. Nice little podcast you run that features killers." He leaned in, voice lowering. "You are exactly what Cal always wanted his son to become."

Damon's heart nearly stopped. "You're lying."

"Am I?" The masked man reached into his coat and tossed something onto the floor at Damon's feet.

An old, faded photograph.

Damon looked down and saw himself. As a child. In his mother's arms. Taken secretly, from across a parking lot.

It wasn't the same one as earlier, but close enough. The photograph trembled in Damon's hand as he picked it up.

The killer didn't budge. "I've known you a very long time."

Damon's breath came in ragged bursts. "If you hurt Ariana—"

"If you don't join me, Damon, I won't just hurt her." The masked man sounded bored, but his voice sharpened into a blade. "I'll kill everyone in this hospital."

Damon's chest exploded with terror.

"Ariana. Wendy. Kaylee. Ed. Reed. Eric." The man listed them casually, like reading names off a grocery list. "One by one. Slowly."

Damon stepped forward, shaking, rage mixing with dread.

"You touch them," he whispered, "and I will—"

"You'll what?" the killer teased. "Lose control? Fall apart? Become the monster your father molded you to be? Good. I want that for you."

Damon's vision swam.

"You have an hour," the man said, turning away, "to decide who lives." He disappeared back into the shadows, footsteps echoing down the corridor.

Damon's legs threatened to give out.

He braced a hand against the wall, heart racing.

"Ari..." he whispered, voice breaking. "I'm coming. I swear, I'm coming."

But now the stakes were blood-soaked and impossible.

Because if Damon chose wrong... he would lose everyone.

Chapter Forty

The bolt loosened one millimeter at a time.

Ariana's muscles burned. Her fingers slipped. The metal wedge cut into her palm until she felt warmth—blood—but she didn't stop.

She couldn't.

The chain groaned, scraping concrete, every sound too loud in the cramped room.

"One more," she whispered, straining with the last of her strength. "Just one more..."

The bolt shifted.

Not all the way. Almost there. Far enough that when she leaned her weight back, the anchor pulled out another half inch.

Hope sparked in her chest. "Come on!"

She braced her foot, grabbed the chain with both hands, and yanked with everything she had left.

The bolt snapped loose.

Ariana stumbled backward, but caught herself, and the

chain slithered free, long enough for her to stand, long enough to reach the door.

She wasn't unbound. But she was mobile.

And that was enough.

Her breath trembled as she staggered to her feet. Assessing the door, she pulled the wedge from her pocket. The door's lock would be impossible to pick—it was heavy, reinforced, designed for isolation.

But the panel over the viewing slit... that could work.

She popped the wedge under the metal cover then pried.

It popped off with a loud clang.

Ariana winced. Froze.

Footsteps?

Nothing.

She climbed up. Peeked out the slit.

A shadowed hallway of linoleum floors, wall rails, and plastic signs with peeling letters stretched into the darkness.

Ariana squinted.

One of the signs was still intact, hanging crooked on the opposite wall.

Maternity nurses' station

Cold poured through her veins like liquid ice.

This wasn't a random storage room. Someone had put her in the maternity ward. Where pregnant patients used to be monitored, where newborns had been kept safe. Someone had brought her where scared mothers-to-be huddled in beds with monitors beeping overhead.

Her hand drifted to her stomach. "Why bring me here?"

She didn't have time to answer herself.

A soft thump echoed down the hall.

Footsteps, shuffling.

Different from before.

Ariana held her breath, peering through the slit again.

A figure stumbled around the corner.

Not the killer.

Marlene.

Her scrubs torn.

Blood smeared across one sleeve.

Hair wild.

Eyes wide and glazed.

Ariana gasped. "Marlene!"

Marlene's head jerked toward the sound. "Ariana? Oh, thank God!"

"Marlene, open the door!"

Marlene staggered to her, fumbling with shaking hands. "He... he tried to stop me. He grabbed me! I thought—"

"Hurry!" Ariana pleaded. "He could come back any minute."

Marlene's fingers found the keyring at her hip. Somehow she still had it, even after whatever the killer had put her through.

She slid the key into the lock.

Turned.

The door swung open.

Ariana lunged forward, chain dragging behind her, nearly collapsing into Marlene's arms. "We have to move! We have to go."

Marlene grabbed her shoulders.

Up close, Ariana saw beneath the eerie calm Marlene had worn all night. She shook so violently her keys rattled in her hand. Her breath came in short, panicked bursts, and her eyes were wide in a way that broke something in Ariana's chest.

"I—I'm sorry," Marlene stammered as she fumbled with the lock. "I know I've been... acting strange all night. I know how I must have looked. But I wasn't hiding anything. I swear I wasn't. I'm not good with fear. When I panic, I... I shut down. I worked here for twenty-three years, and after the shutdown—after everything that happened—coming back felt like walking through a grave I thought I'd buried." She shot a terrified look down the hall, then back at Ariana. "I wasn't following anyone. I wasn't trying to scare anyone. I just..." Her voice cracked. "I was trying to make sure no one died on my watch again."

Ariana's breath hitched.

Marlene turned it with a trembling, relieved sob. "I heard you screaming. I heard him dragging something and I thought it was already too late." Marlene clutched her with surprising strength—protective, desperate, nothing like the cold figure the group had feared. She breathed against Ari's shoulder. "I'm sorry. I'm so sorry. I should've spoken up sooner. I should've told all of you what I knew."

Ariana pulled back just enough to see her face. It was tear-streaked, afraid, but absolutely on their side. "Right now all that matters is getting out of here."

Marlene nodded quickly, wiping her face with her sleeve. "Then let's go, before he comes back."

A metallic crash sounded at the end of the hall.

Both women jerked toward the noise.

Ariana grabbed Marlene's arm. "We have to go *now*!"

But before they could take a single step, footsteps rounded the corner.

Coming straight for them.

Ariana pulled Marlene behind her, ready to run, ready to fight, ready to do whatever it took.

The footsteps echoed closer—measured, steady.

Ariana's pulse roared in her ears.

"Go," she whispered to Marlene. "Now. Move."

Marlene nodded, white-faced.

They slipped out of the doorway just as another footstep landed. Then another.

Ariana grabbed Marlene's wrist and pulled her down the hall.

The maternity wing stretched in both directions, long and dim, walls lined with faded murals of cartoon giraffes and smiling storks. Their cheerful pastel colors felt grotesque now, warped by flickering light and the shadow of a killer walking calmly toward them.

Ariana's chain clattered behind her, dragging unevenly across tile. She picked it up so it wouldn't make any more noise.

"Wait," Marlene hissed.

"Not now."

They rounded a corner.

A soft, amused hum echoed behind them.

He was following.

Ariana's skin crawled.

The hallway forked. Left went toward the old neonatal rooms, right toward the nurses' lounge. Signs hung crooked, half-ripped from the walls.

Safety could've been anywhere.

"Left." Marlene pulled Ariana with her.

They pushed through a door marked INFANT OBSERVATION, slipping into a long room with empty bassinets lined in rows.

Ariana's breath caught. Something felt wrong.

Like someone else was in there.

"One of the windows," Marlene whispers desperately. "They used to open them for ventilation. If we can pry one..."

A metallic click came from the doorway.

Marlene froze.

Ariana turned slowly, bile rising.

The masked man loomed in the door.

He blocked the only exit. "You shouldn't have come out so soon."

Ariana stepped in front of Marlene. "You stay away from her."

"Brave," he murmured. "But misguided."

Ariana's heart hammered.

"Marlene," she whispered without looking back. "Find a window."

Marlene started for the far end of the room.

The masked man watched with mild interest. "She won't get far."

Ariana snatched the nearest thing she could reach. A cracked bassinet lid, and she held it like a shield.

The man chuckled. "You're protecting the nurse? Sweet. But I'm only interested in you."

Ariana's stomach lurched. "What do you want?"

He took another step toward her. "Damon is what I'm here for."

Ariana's veins turned to ice. "He isn't like his father."

The man's laugh sliced the air. "You think love saved him? You think you saved him?"

Ariana tightened her grip on the bassinet lid. "I know I did."

The man stopped. "You're wrong. He's still Cal's son."

She threw the lid at his face.

He staggered, surprised but not stunned.

Ariana whirled and bolted toward Marlene, who shoved up on a partially stuck window. It opened an inch, two inches…

Footsteps shuffled as the man charged toward them.

Ariana grabbed the bassinet itself this time, the whole metal frame. She shoved it backward, sending it crashing into his legs.

He stumbled, falling against another bassinet behind him.

"Go!" Ariana yelled.

Marlene dove through the narrow opening.

Ariana dropped low, crouching to follow her.

But the chain snagged. Yanked her hard.

She stumbled.

The masked man lunged.

A bassinet toppled over, landing on the floor. Skidded toward Ariana's legs.

Her hands scrambled for the chain. Pulling, twisting, trying to free it.

His hand closed on her ankle. Her cuff. He dragged her backward.

Ariana screamed.

Marlene's hands latched around her wrists from outside the window.

Ari braced her feet. The cuff dug into her skin.

The man's grip tightened.

A loud metallic crack split the struggle.

The bolt on the chain gave way.

Ariana flew forward, nearly crashing into the window frame, catching herself just in time.

She and Marlene stumbled into a narrow exterior walkway. Her feet slipped on frost. The bitter air bit through her clothes, stung her cheeks.

Behind them, the masked man crashed into the window frame, shattering what little glass remained.

Ariana ran.

Chapter Forty-One

A violent metallic clatter sounded, making Damon's heart stop. It was followed by a distorted thud and a woman's scream. Undeniably Ariana's scream.

He shouted for her, sprinting toward the noise, his flashlight beam jerking wildly across the walls.

Everything around him became a blur. Damon cut a corner so sharply his shoulder hit the wall.

Then, through an open doorway, he saw movement.

The masked man.

Dragging something. Someone.

Rage shot through Damon like wildfire.

He launched himself forward.

The man looked up just as Damon shoved into him with the full weight of a man who'd already decided he didn't care if he lived or died as long as his wife survived.

They crashed into a row of empty bassinets, metal frames clattering across the tile.

The masked man snarled beneath the distortion of his altered voice. "I told you not to make this harder."

Hide and Seek

Damon hit him again, driving a fist into the man's jaw so hard his own knuckles screamed.

"Don't you touch her! You don't even look at her!"

The man twisted, faster than Damon expected, swinging an elbow into Damon's ribs.

Damon buckled but didn't fall. He grabbed the man by the collar, drove him back into the wall.

The mask slipped, revealing a glimpse of pale skin and a cruel smirk.

"You're proving me right," the killer hissed. "Just like him. Just like Cal."

Damon's vision went red.

He punched again, harder. The man's head snapped sideways.

The killer's head lolled for a heartbeat, but then he started laughing. Not normal laughter. A jagged, broken sound that reminded him of a wild animal. He stared at Damon with sheer delight. "There it *is*. The fire! You have the instinct."

"What are you talking about?" Damon's pulse thundered, but the man only leaned closer.

"You think Cal was just a murderer?" he rasped. "You think he was some mindless beast? No, he was *building* something. He was teaching us how to transcend all this." He waved a trembling hand at the hospital walls, the snowstorm beyond, the entire fragile world. "He was showing us what we're capable of when we stop pretending to be tame."

Damon blinked a few times. "You're as crazy as he was."

His voice pitched high suddenly, hysterical. "And you." He jabbed a finger at Damon's chest. "You were his *masterpiece*! His greatest work. The one thing he couldn't finish before they stole him away!"

The man clutched his mask with both hands, shaking with fervor. "I spent years studying him. Years learning every step, every symbol, every ritual he practiced. But I couldn't continue his work alone. I need the bloodline. You're the key—the son who carries his genius in his bones."

Damon shook his head. "You're wrong."

He let his hands drop, revealing a wild, gleeful grin beneath the cracked mask. "You feel it, don't you? The heat under your skin. The pull toward violence. The part of you that *enjoyed* hitting me just now."

Damon's breath hitched.

The killer's expression softened with twisted affection. "Oh, Damon, Cal always said you'd be extraordinary. That you'd eclipse him. And once you join me, we'll finish what he started. The world won't know what's coming."

"You... you *knew* him?" Damon sputtered.

"He was my mentor." The man leaned forward, his voice dipping into a conspiratorial whisper. "It won't be complete without you. It could *never* be complete without you. You're the heir. The crown. You're the ending to his story."

His laugh returned, shooing sanity out of the air like a flock of birds scattering to the dark. "And the beginning of mine."

Damon came to his senses and hit the man again. His fist hit the killer's jaw with such force, he both heard and felt the crack.

But the killer was quick, and he swept Damon's legs out from under him.

Damon crashed onto the tile, breath exploding from his lungs.

"Damon!" Ariana's voice.

Ariana.

He twisted, searching. "Did you... Are you...?"

She stood outside, peering through a cracked window at the far end of the room, Marlene next to her.

Alive.

She was still alive.

Ariana started to climb through, back into danger.

The killer lunged toward the window.

"Ari, no!" Damon grabbed the man's coat then yanked him backward with a roar. "You're not touching her!"

They grappled, bodies crashing against overturned bassinets. The man swung a metal pole toward Damon's head. Damon ducked, grabbed his arm, twisted with all the fury he had.

The pole flew out of the killer's hand and clanged across the floor.

A split second of imbalance.

Damon didn't waste it. He drove the man back into the supply cabinet, metal denting under the force of the impact.

But the killer recovered fast. Faster than Damon could track, and his gloved fist slammed into Damon's stomach, knocking him backward.

Damon hit the ground hard, groaning.

The killer stepped toward him, breathing too steady. "You don't have a choice, Damon. You join me, or they all die. Starting with her."

Clang!

A heavy metal bar crashed against the man's shoulder. He staggered.

Ariana stood in the open walkway, gripping part of a broken bassinet frame like a weapon. Her breath came in sharp, terrified bursts, but her eyes were fierce. "Stay away from him!"

The killer recovered, turning toward her.

Damon's rage surged white-hot.

He grabbed the metal pole and swung.

It smashed into the killer's ribs with a hollow crack.

The man crumpled sideways, mask scraping the tile as his

head hit the floor. He wasn't unconscious, but dazed. At least enough to buy them a few seconds.

"Go!" Damon shouted at Ariana. "Run!"

She reached for him instead, eyes shining with panic. "I'm not leaving you."

He took her hand in one swift, desperate grip. "Then move."

The masked man pushed himself up on unsteady arms. He lunged for Ariana, who stumbled backward. He lunged again, wild now, no longer patient or controlled.

Damon caught her around the waist, pulled her behind him, then braced for another hit.

Marlene yanked open a heavy steel utility closet door beside her. "Hurry! Push him in!"

The killer spun toward her. Damon rammed his shoulder into the man's chest. The impact sent them both crashing into the closet's threshold.

Ariana grabbed the killer's coat sleeve with trembling hands, adding every ounce of her strength to Damon's momentum.

The man snarled behind his mask. "You really think you can—"

Damon cut him off with another shove, this one fueled by pure terror and fury. The killer lost his footing on the cluttered floor inside the closet. He slid over bundled mops and old plastic containers.

Marlene landed against the closet door.

Hard.

The masked man hit it from the inside, and the door shuddered.

"Lock it!" Damon barked.

Ariana scrambled, fingers flying over the latch. "It's stuck!"

"Move!" Damon grabbed the bent latch with both hands

then heaved downward. It screeched but held, sliding into place with a heavy, final clunk.

A beat of silence.

Then a roar from inside the closet, so full of rage it shook the air.

Marlene backed up until she hit the opposite wall, eyes wide.

Ariana leaned into Damon, breath coming fast and thin. "He's not staying in there long."

"No," Damon said, voice low, grim. "But it's long enough."

Marlene shoved some equipment in front of the door. "That'll help. Hopefully until the authorities can get here."

"Thank you." Damon grabbed Ariana's hand.

"Don't thank me yet. There isn't any cell service. We'll have to figure out how to contact the cops."

Together, they fled down the hall.

Damon didn't look back.

He wrapped his arm around Ariana's shoulders as they bolted down the corridor, Marlene stumbling ahead of them.

Ed shouted their names from farther down the hall. Other voices sounded too.

They were close to finding the rest of the group.

And most importantly, Damon had proven he wasn't like his father. He'd had the chance to kill, but he'd refused. Locked the man up, and assuming he stayed in the closet until the police arrived, he would go to jail for a long, long time.

Chapter Forty Two

Wendy had never expected morning to come. Not after the night they'd lived through—the screams, the running, the death, the fear. She'd never been so terrified Kaylee might not survive a single night.

But morning came anyway. Ed had taken a shortcut through the woods he knew and found a phone to call the authorities.

Cold gray light filtered through the hospital's shattered front window, mixing with the flash of police lights outside. Officers moved through the lobby in practiced formations, collecting statements, photographing damage, escorting paramedics down hallways Wendy never wanted to see again.

The killer, whose rage simmered in his expression, stopped as he passed Damon. "You really think stopping me will change anything? I'm not working alone. And when he comes... he'll finish everything we started. He'll come for you, Damon. He'll never leave you alone."

Wendy and Damon exchanged a worried look. Ariana was talking with an officer, so she hadn't heard that. For that,

Wendy was glad. She gave Damon a sympathetic glance. "I'm sure he was just blowing hot air."

He nodded. "Right. Trying to get under my skin."

"Exactly."

One of the attending officers shoved the killer forward, and once outside, he was locked into a squad car. It took three officers to force him in.

Wendy didn't look away until the car door closed.

Only then did she exhale, shoulders sagging.

Kaylee squeezed her hand. "It's over, Mom."

Wendy brushed hair from her daughter's face. "Finally."

An officer approached with a gentle smile. "Ma'am? We need just a few more details for the report."

Wendy answered what she could, giving times, the direction they ran, where she last saw Marlene before she fled with Ariana. That fear had carved itself into her bones.

Kaylee stuck close while officers came and went. Ariana, pale and shaken but alive, leaned on Damon's shoulder as paramedics checked her ankle. Damon hovered like he was ready to carry her out of the building if they so much as suggested he leave her side.

Wendy watched the two of them quietly. There was something about the way Damon held her in a gentle but intense way that made Wendy's chest tighten. She'd been so suspicious of them, and now she understood fear born from love. Maybe she always had.

After a while, Eric stepped beside her. His face was pale with exhaustion, eyes rimmed red. Not from tears, but from years of hiding them. Years of being pulled in two directions— fear of Cal and fear of what the truth might cost him.

He cleared his throat. "I already told the officers everything," he said softly. "Everything I should have told you years ago."

Wendy studied him. Really studied him. For the first time in a long time, she saw the kid he must've been. The terrified teenager trapped by a monster, forced into silence. Not a coward, not inattentive. Just... traumatized.

"Wendy," he said, voice shaking, "about the divorce. I'll make it easy. No arguments, or fight. You deserve the best. I'm sorry I couldn't give it to you."

She put a hand up.

He froze.

Kaylee drifted a few feet away to sit beside Ariana, exhausted enough to lean against her.

Wendy drew in a deep breath. "Eric, I thought our marriage was failing because you didn't care anymore. Because you weren't trying."

"I *wasn't* trying," he whispered. "I didn't know how. And for that, I'm sorry."

She nodded slowly. "You were dealing with something I didn't understand. Something you never gave me the chance to understand."

His shoulders slumped. "I know. That's on me. I was ashamed. Afraid you'd think I was... like him."

Wendy stepped closer. "You're nothing like him."

He closed his eyes, breath catching.

"And now," she continued gently, "I know why. I know what he did to you. What he threatened. How you lived."

He opened his eyes again, stunned. "Wendy, after everything, you couldn't possibly still want a life with me."

"I want to try. To give us one more chance."

Eric blinked in disbelief. "You... you do?"

"I'm not pretending everything's fine," she added. "It's not. And we have a lot to work through. A *lot*. But now that I understand the truth, I don't want to abandon you. Not when you finally told me."

Eric covered his face with both hands, shaking with a quiet, broken exhale.

Wendy put her hand on his shoulder.

"We'll do counseling," she said. "All of us. Family therapy, trauma therapy. Whatever it takes."

He nodded, tears shining in his eyes.

"And we do it together. If you want that."

Eric looked at her then with an expression she hadn't seen in years. Not desperation or guilt.

Belief.

"I want that more than anything."

Wendy squeezed his hand.

Kaylee watched them from across the room, eyes tired but hopeful.

Outside, the officers drove the killer away. Inside, the survivors gathered their things.

Ariana and Damon shared a quiet embrace.

Marlene sat with paramedics, answering questions.

Reed paced by the entrance, arguing with a deputy.

Wendy held her family close.

And, for the first time since the storm began, she let herself believe they would be okay.

Chapter Forty-Three

Ariana leaned back in the passenger seat, wrapped in a soft blanket a paramedic had insisted she take. Snow still clung to the mountains as Damon steered the SUV down the newly plowed highway, the storm a distant memory now, shrinking in the rearview mirror. Morning sunlight turned the snowbanks gold, warm despite the cold outside.

Damon kept glancing over at her like he couldn't quite believe she was real.

She smiled back every time, reassuring him.

Her sore ankle was wrapped, her aching body exhausted, and her nerves still raw in places she didn't want to touch yet, but she was alive. They both were.

"You okay?" Damon asked, voice quiet and careful.

Ariana nodded, brushing her thumb over the folded blanket. "I'm doing great, considering. Tired, sore, but grateful." She let out a breath. "Really grateful."

Damon's hand found hers across the console, fingers weaving through hers like they'd been waiting for this moment. His grip was steady and warm. Familiar and comforting.

"I keep thinking," he said, eyes on the road, "that if I'd been faster, or smarter, or—"

"Damon." She squeezed his hand. "You saved me. More than once."

He didn't answer right away. His jaw worked, the faintest tremor in the muscle there. "I thought I was going to lose you. I was terrified this would be the end, after everything we've already been through."

Ariana reached over and ran her fingers through his hair gently. "I knew you'd find me. I held onto that the whole time."

"Marlene found you first."

"You still found me."

He glanced at her then for just a second, but full of so much emotion she felt her heart ache.

"You shouldn't have had to go through any of that. Most of the bad things you've been through have been because of me."

"Not you. Your father. That's a big difference."

"I'm half him."

She shook her head. "You're who you choose to be. And I happen to be extremely fond of that person."

"Still, you've been through more than you ever should have."

"Maybe so, but I wouldn't change a thing. You're worth all of it."

"Everything? Multiple abductions? Threats on your life?"

"You can't pretend I hadn't already gone through all of that long before ever meeting you. We both have our own traumas. Maybe that's why we work so well together."

He let out a breath, long and shaky. She knew he was replaying everything. His father's shadow, the killer's taunts, the decisions he was forced to make. But the fear that usually followed wasn't in his eyes now. Something steadier was replacing it.

Hope.

They passed the sign for the mountain range, the one they'd been driving through before everything went wrong. Damon reached over to adjust the heater and Ariana noticed how his hands no longer shook.

"Once we get home," she said, voice soft, "I want to start therapy again. For everything that happened. For... before."

He nodded. "Yeah. I want that too."

She rested a hand on her stomach. "And I want us to raise this baby without fear. Without secrets."

Damon's eyes softened. "None at all."

They drove another mile in quiet, the good kind of quiet, filled with breath and warmth and sunlight and healing.

The mountains gave way to rolling hills, and Ariana felt the first true wave of peace settle over her. The nightmare behind them. The future ahead.

Damon glanced at her again, his smile small but real. "You know," he said lightly, "before they hauled him off, he tried to rattle me. Said some garbage about not working alone. About someone else 'continuing the mission.'"

Ariana's fingers tightened into fists. "You didn't think to mention that sooner?"

Damon shrugged like it meant nothing. "Classic last-ditch scare tactic. Guys like that can't stand losing, so they spit threats. It's all talk."

Ariana didn't answer right away. She watched the snow blur past the window, thoughtful. "Are you sure? That was really the feeling you got from him?"

"Positive. We're going to be fine."

She drew in a deep breath. "I hope so."

Damon kept his smile, and Ariana leaned back in her seat,

trying to let the warmth of his expression reassure her. Trying to believe him.

But long after Damon faced the road again, she still stared ahead, heart beating just slightly faster.

Because sometimes threats were just threats.

And sometimes... they weren't.

Damon and Ariana's next book: Last One Standing.

Books by Stacy Claflin

PSYCHOLOGICAL THRILLERS

Brannon House

The Perfect Death

Family Secrets

The Darkest Garden

Shattered Pieces

Grave Memories

Drowning Silence

Sleepwalker

Face Off

Lost Echoes

The Watcher

Her Last Breath

Secrets We Hide

No Safe Place

Ariana Jones

Watch Your Back

Don't Look Now

Without a Trace

Never Letting Go

Lie in Wait

No Way Out

Hide and Seek

Last One Standing

Alex Mercer Thrillers

Girl in Trouble

Turn Back Time

Little Lies

Against All Odds

Don't Forget Me

Tainted Love

Take On Me

Danger Zone

Lady in Red

White Wedding

Careless Whisper

Never Surrender

The Gone Saga

The Gone Trilogy: Gone, Held, Over

Dean's List

No Return

Recluse Island

The Hotel's Secret

The Father's Secret

The Corpse's Secret

Thriller Standalones

Don't Trust Her
Lies Never Sleep
Lost and Found

FANTASY

Sisterhood of Midlife Magic
You've Got Magic
Spell-less in Seattle
Impractical Magic

Legacy of the Hunter
The Secret Keeper's Daughter
The Midnight Death Match

Dark Sea Academy
Mermaid's Song
Mermaid's Heart
Mermaid's Wish

Curse of the Moon
Lost Wolf
Chosen Wolf
Hunted Wolf
Broken Wolf
Cursed Wolf
Secret Jaguar

Valhalla's Curse
Renegade Valkyrie

Pursued Valkyrie
Silenced Valkyrie
Vengeful Valkyrie
Unleashed Valkyrie

The Transformed Series

Deception
Betrayal
Forgotten
Ascension
Duplicity
Sacrifice
Destroyed
Transcend
Entangled
Dauntless
Obscured
Partition

Side Stories:

Fallen
Silent Bite
Hidden Intentions
Saved by a Vampire
Sweet Desire

Paranormal Standalones

Dex

Beauty

Haunted

EMOTIONAL ROMANCE

Flawed Souls

When Tomorrow Starts Without Me

The Only Things You Can Take

When You Start to Miss Me

FAMILY SAGA ROMANCE

The Hunters

Seaside Surprises

Seaside Heartbeats

Seaside Dances

Seaside Kisses

Seaside Christmas

Bayside Wishes

Bayside Evenings

Bayside Promises

Bayside Destinies

Bayside Opposites

Bayside Mistletoe

Bayside Dreams

SHARED WORLD ROMANCES

Indigo Bay Romances

Sweet Dreams

Sweet Reunion

Sweet Complications

Fall into Romance

Lost in Romance

ROMANTIC COMEDIES

(Writing under the pen name Eden Bloom)

Misty Falls Romantic Comedies

Yoga One For Me

All I Want For Christmas is Ewe

Must Love Cats

Happily Ever Laughter

SHORT STORIES

Tiny Bites Collection

COWRITTEN BOOKS

Dead for Good series

Dead for Good

Left for Dead

Dead of Night

Wake the Dead

Dead for Life

About Stacy Claflin

Stacy Claflin is a *USA Today* bestselling thriller author who has published more than 100 novels, including Girl in Trouble and The Perfect Death. She has always been curious about the human mind, and in her quest to learn more, she earned a degree in Psychology. Her favorite course was Abnormal Behavior, which has been useful in writing fiction.

Her love for thrillers goes back to her early childhood when she fell in love with Unsolved Mysteries and America's Most Wanted. When Stacy was five, she got mad at a babysitter who wouldn't let her watch the evening news. These days, she spends her free time listening to true crime podcasts or watching documentaries on the subject.

She has been telling stories for as long as she can remember, and as child would often get into trouble for trying to convince friends her wild tales were true. Now she puts her creativity to better use by writing page-turning stories that leave readers begging for more.

Stacy occasionally dabbles in other genres, so as you peruse her library of works, you'll find some romance and paranormal tales, all with strong suspense elements.

For more information:
stacyclaflin.com/about

Find Me

I'd love to connect with you!

Find me on any or all of the following sites. I'm not equally active everywhere, but I'd love to meet you where you love to hang out.

Email: https://stacyclaflin.com/newsletter
I send my newsletter once a week or every other week, and include book updates, new release alerts, freebie notifications, and more. Sometimes I send cat pictures and share interesting facts about my books.

Website: https://stacyclaflin.com/
Find out more about my books on my website. I've written over 80 novels, so chances are, you'll find some books you didn't know about before.

Bookbub: https://www.bookbub.com/authors/stacy-claflin
Bookbub is where I share, rate, and review books that I've

read. You can also get new release and pre-order alerts if you follow me there.

Facebook: https://www.facebook.com/stacy.claflin.author/

Facebook is a huge time suck for me, so I try not to spend too much time there. (I get a lot more writing done that way!) But you can follow me for book updates. I also have a street team you can join: https://www.facebook.com/groups/StacyClaflinStreetTeam/

TikTok:

Thriller books: https://www.tiktok.com/@stacyclaflin
Fantasy books: https://www.tiktok.com/@stacy.claflin

Pinterest: https://www.pinterest.com/growwithstacy/_saved/

I used to be really active on Pinterest, so there are a lot of fun boards, but I don't update them often. If you like Pinterest, you might enjoy browsing my profile. Just don't expect many updates!

Instagram: https://www.instagram.com/stacy.claflin/

I'm not super active on Instagram, but I do try to put book updates and pretty pictures when I think about it.

Printed in Dunstable, United Kingdom